# Illusion Razed

## Gwydion Royce

ORACLE OF LOST PATHS BOOKS

Cover Design by Damonza.com

1st edition 2024

Oracle of Lost Paths Books

author@gwydionroyce.com

979-8-9902074-6-2 (eBook)

979-8-9902074-7-9 (Paperback)

# CHAPTER ONE

# Meg

Catapulting through time is an art form as much as dumb luck. It takes a while to learn, but once you've got a handle on pinpointing your destination, it's easy to stick the landing. At least, I'd never had a problem with it before.

Now, as Gareth and I looked around us at the miles of ocean between us and the next island, there was no question that I'd missed the mark.

"Where are we?" asked Gareth.

I shook my head. "I was aiming for Athens. This isn't it."

We were on a coast overlooking a natural harbor. A small settlement nearby bustled with activity, and in the distance, goats were being herded toward the grassy plains. Mountains in the west rose proudly, bathed in the early morning sun. When the wind blew just right, the voices of the hawkers within the city walls drifted toward us as they enticed buyers. They were speaking a dialect of Ancient Greek, so at least we were in the correct region.

Gareth made a noise and turned to me with excitement. "I can understand them. That man was naming off foods, wasn't he?"

"Yes." I laughed, just as thrilled as he was about this development. "You must've got my gift of language when we bonded."

Heat flashed in his eyes and his hands rested on my hips. He leaned down and spoke into my ear. "I know we're running from an angry god on the warpath, but I'm looking forward to deepening our connection."

His emotions rolled through me as if they were my own, but instead of a matching fire rising within me, it was anxiety that churned my stomach. Gareth pulled me close, bathing me in his stoic calm. "What's wrong?"

"I—" How could I explain it without hurting him? I knew to expect the sharing of senses and emotions, but it was an odd experience. It almost made me uncomfortable, to be that vulnerable to someone else.

"It's hard to describe," I said, lamely. A hum rumbled up from Gareth's chest and I glanced at him. The look of knowing said it all. "And I don't need to, because you already sensed it."

He kissed the top of my head. "Aye. You have every right to be nervous. Being this open to you is taking a toll on me, as well. Even where the other Six were concerned, I was never an open book. It'll take adjusting to." He smiled down at me. "I'm right here with you. Exactly where I belong."

"I apologize in advance for anything inappropriate I may send through the bond," I said, face buried in his chest, already expecting embarrassing moments.

Gareth growled. "Don't be. I plan on bombarding you with naughty thoughts every chance I get."

He leaned in to nibble at my ear, and I put a hand on his chest. "Angry god chasing us, remember?"

"Right," he sighed. Most of the island that we could see wasn't ideal for hiding. Low scrub and beach grass covered most of the surrounding area that wasn't just sand or hard rock.

"We can shift," said Gareth. His eyes lit up with pride. "We were going to go for a run. I want to see your new form."

Excitement overrode my worries. In all the rush of running from Bel, my new ability had slipped my mind. "We could." I gave him a wry smile. "But it feels like that would only draw more attention, not less."

Gareth shrugged. "Perhaps. We'll be faster than any aggressors though."

I was still hesitant.

Once again, his calm surfaced and brushed against my mind. "Do you feel any immediate danger?" he asked.

I stilled, reaching out into time, testing for any disruptions. Whenever someone made waves through time by trying to force their way through it like Bel did, the resulting ripples travelled for a long way, like dropping a rock in a pond. You could usually tell which way the intruder was heading long before they got there... but everything was still.

I opened my mouth to answer, but there was a sudden jolt on the edge of my consciousness. Like someone was trying to take a peek into my head.

"What is it?" asked Gareth.

My brow furrowed. From the corner of my eye, I thought I saw a dark figure standing on a rocky outcrop, wearing robes that were billowing in the stiff wind. When I looked at that spot, full view, the figure was gone.

"I thought I saw something, there." I pointed.

Gareth looked where I was pointing but shook his head. "I don't see anything."

"Take a look out of the corner of your eye and see if it changes."

He did as I asked and scanned for a bit, but shrugged. "Still nothing."

"Hmm. Did you feel anything? Like, in your head?"

"How do you mean?" His fists clenched, and through the bond, I knew he was on edge that I'd sensed a danger he hadn't.

"Almost like a fuzzy or swimming sensation?"

"No. Nothing like that." He frowned, the muscles in his arms cording. "What do you think it is?"

"I don't know." I paused. "Maybe it was nothing. I'm just being hypervigilant."

"And Belsioch? Anything from him?"

I shook my head. "No, not yet. It would've taken a lot of energy for him to force his way through time so if he got through, he'll need time to recover."

"Then we'll use that head start to explore the island, figure out where we are and let you get to know your wolf." His tone became serious. "The sooner you make the shift, the better. It'll help you forge a close bond with your instincts. Your wolf will always do her best to watch your back, even if you yourself aren't paying attention."

Nerves set my stomach fluttering, and Gareth smiled, boyish and happy.

"Okay. Walk me through it."

Gareth held out his hand, and I took it. That rush of power that he'd used to coax my wolf forward in the cave swooped over me again, stronger this time. I braced myself for the pain of the shift, but there wasn't any. Instead, pressure pushed at me from all sides, molding my shape into something else with gentle hands.

A nuzzle against my face made me open my eyes.

And the world had changed.

After the bonding, my eyesight had been sharper, colors a little more vivid, but now everything was amped up to eleven. It reminded me of the few occasions I'd visited the Strangefells with Bel. Hypersaturation, to the point of straining my vision.

The scent of the goats we'd seen earlier wafted toward me on the breeze and I turned, ready to run after them, my mouth salivating. Claws dug into the sand under my paws as my back legs bunched and readied to spring.

Teeth closed around the scruff of my neck and bit down just enough to bring me back to awareness. I relaxed my muscles, and the teeth released me.

Gareth's black wolf was staring at me out of yellow eyes. He was still bigger than me in wolf form, but not by much.

I padded over to the water, surrounded by the noise of roaring waves crashing outside the harbor, and gulls flying overhead with piercing shrieks. The calls from the vendors in the city, the goats braying, the hammering of mallets on stone somewhere within the walls, those damn gulls. Every sound I became conscious of ratcheted up in volume until I was surrounded by deafening noise that blended together into a painful cacophony. I whined and pawed at my ears, lowering my belly to the ground.

Gareth was beside me then, pressing his massive wolf form against me. I leaned into him and regained control as his wolf spoke to mine, soothing her. The sounds faded to tolerable, and a few minutes after that, returned to normal.

I nuzzled my face against his in thanks and continued toward the water. It was calm enough in the harbor that I could see my reflection. A small yip escaped my throat as I saw my wolf for the first time.

Staring back at me was a silver wolf with a black undercoat, with black-tipped ears and tail. My eyes were still bright violet.

I lifted my head and found Gareth staring at me, eyes soft and loving. With a sharp bark, he took off running, and I gave chase. My legs tangled, and I went sprawling, eating sand. Rough grains got stuck in my nostrils and I sneezed. Gareth had stopped on a rocky outcrop and barked, a teasing grin on his face. His tongue lolled out of his mouth before he disappeared, barely making any sound as he ran.

Growling and carefully climbing to my four feet, I jogged to get used to the gait. As soon as I felt confident in my steps, I took off after him, gaining ground in no time. The wind rushing through my fur was exhilarating. He kept rounding corners out of sight ahead of me, so I homed in on his scent and let that guide my feet. His tail disappeared around a boulder only seconds before I got there.

As I turned the corner, Gareth barreled into me, and we went rolling. We scuffled, yipping and nipping at each other until I got a piece of him, pinching the skin under his front leg with my teeth, right in the sensitive part of his armpit. Not hard enough to draw blood, but enough to make him take notice.

He yelped, and I gleefully bounded away. Surprise was evident on his face before he schooled it and took a firm stance as we faced each other. There was a gleam in his eye, and Gareth charged me, but I surprised him again by running right at him and leaping over and away, tearing off toward the distant mountains.

Gareth tried to catch me up, but he wasn't fast enough. I raced ahead, bothered by nothing, the wind in my face and the cadence of my paws on the ground keeping a steady rhythm. Once the adrenaline of the run evened out, I slowed, giving him a chance. He ambled up alongside me and nuzzled my neck before we fell into an easy gait and explored the island.

The terrain was diverse. Mountains, arid desert, grassy plains, surrounded by a sparkling blue ocean with several other islands in the distance, ever present but a world away. After hours of exploring in this fashion, we found a patch of shade, the blistering sun beating down on us. We stopped at a cistern and lapped up the cool, fresh water before we curled up around each other and dozed off. My last conscious thought was of how happy I felt in that moment and how Gareth felt the same.

I woke up to Gareth's breathing on my face. My wolf eyes opened to find him crouched down in front of me, also still in wolf form, tail swishing over the beach grass and staring at me intently. His mouth cracked in a smile when he saw I was awake.

I got to my four legs and shook my body, working out the stiffness from the run. It had been more of a workout than I'd expected, breaking in a new form. My head felt a little fuzzy, and I tried to clear it with another cold drink from the cistern, but it didn't work. I tried to shake it off one more time but decided that another run with Gareth would do the trick.

On the other side of the island from where we'd landed, there wasn't a beach as much as rocky tidal shoals, filled with all sorts of barnacles and mussels clinging to the rocks. Volcanic islands were guaranteed to have caves and, sure enough, we found an entrance to one that delved deep underground and into pure darkness.

My head was pounding, and I felt so tired, but Gareth forged ahead into the cave. I followed.

The tunnels ran underneath the island a considerable way. We'd been padding along for at least an hour, winding our way deeper, navigating on scent and sound alone. Even my enhanced vision couldn't make out more than blurry shapes after we were a hundred feet into the tunnel. The absolute void of light was consuming. If Gareth hadn't been with me, I might've lost my mind.

It brought back memories of the labyrinth and the minotaur waiting for me at the center, by its obsidian altar.

Gareth exuded the same steadiness as always, as he led the way forward. He would occasionally fall back and walk shoulder to shoulder with me when he could sense me getting anxious or claustrophobic.

Another thirty minutes, an hour? Even my concept of time was failing, between the darkness and the pounding in my head, a small amount of light came into focus. We headed toward it, and at first I thought we'd found the exit. Then I recognized the orange glow of fire.

I stopped. Why would there be a fire lit this deep into the caves? Gareth stepped back beside me again and I breathed him in. I saw the glimmer of his eyes in the weak glow of the firelight.

*Trust me*, they said.

I followed close behind, heart thudding, as we crept forward. The light grew brighter, and I could feel the heat radiating from the cavern ahead. It made the damp cold we'd been walking through more notable and the stone under my paws was biting with the chill.

A massive shape moved in front of the fire and cast a long, creeping shadow toward us that swept across the walls. My ears twitched forward as the heavy footsteps stopped and metal rasped against metal before a loud clang startled me enough to make me yelp.

The thing in the cave didn't seem to notice and continued hammering against an anvil. Gareth had moved up ahead, and I scurried to follow, not wanting to lose sight of him around any of the many turns.

Sticking to his side, we kept edging forward until we were facing a smoothed archway cut into the rock. Soot had gathered on the walls and ceiling, leaving a grimy residue that overwhelmed me with its acrid scent the closer we got. The chamber we were facing was blistering hot, sparks rising from the anvil as a giant of a man hammered at a blazing red piece of metal.

His body was twisted, face contorted, the misshapen features partially hidden behind a bushy, unkempt beard. He hadn't noticed that we were there.

Gareth took a few more tentative steps into the chamber, his fur blending with the shadows. He kicked a piece of scrap on the floor and the blacksmith paused, peering past the edges of the firelight from the giant forge behind him, not seeing the wolf hiding just out of view.

When the smith went back to his task, Gareth nodded his head for me to follow. Everything was screaming at me not too. I froze to the spot. Gareth slunk back over to me and nudged me forward, but I dug my heels in. This wasn't right. Nothing about this was right. Why did my head hurt so much?

He stared at me hard, and my vision blurred, but not so much that I couldn't see his bared teeth gleaming. The sudden change in him shook me, but I still refused to move. His patience broke, and he snarled, grabbing my neck with his teeth and tossing me into the chamber.

# Chapter Two

# Meg

I scrambled up and tried to run, but a chain shot out from the dark corners of the room and wrapped around me tight. I struggled, panic forcing me out of my wolf form. I still couldn't slip them in human form, and the heavy links of iron immobilized me. The pain was terrible, second only to the piercing throb between my eyes.

"Gareth, help!" I cried, my plea ricocheting around the room. Gareth strode forward calmly, also in human form. He looked at the smith and smiled.

"We've got her."

"What? Gareth, what are you—"

"You thought I was in love with you? That I'd pledge undying loyalty to a frail thing that's helpless without stealing power from others?"

Any words I might've said dried up in my throat.

The giant smith took two steps, towering over me, an evil grin revealing chipped and stained teeth peeking from his unruly beard. His voice rumbled with a bass so low I could barely understand him.

"The Titans will finally have their sacrifice."

"Sacrifice? What?" My voice went up an octave from fear, and I struggled against the bindings.

Gareth knelt down beside me. "You are the key, Meg. Unfortunately for you, the key needs to be forged. From your flesh."

I stared in horror at Gareth and the giant. The god. "Hephaestus?" I asked.

The smith nodded, grinning wider.

"I don't understand," I whispered. "Please, Gareth."

Gareth laughed and mocked me in a high-pitched voice, clasping his hands together. "Please, Gareth." He scowled. "It didn't have to come to this, if you hadn't taken so long to find us. You're worthless in the Titans' original plans. They had to rethink their options." He smiled, all traces of that kind man disappearing in an instant. How was I fooled? Again? It had been too good to be true.

"We need your bones and blood to make the key that will break our masters out of Tartarus. They'll take their rightful places on thrones made of corpses as they rebuild the world from its ashes."

"No." My words were little more than a whimper. A blinding pain shot through my head and my vision clouded with spots.

"Don't worry," he said with a smile. "You won't be around to see it."

"This isn't real," I said, closing my eyes tight. "This isn't real. I'm being manipulated."

Hephaestus handed Gareth a hammer, the gleam of madness in the shifter's eyes stopping my heart. "Where would you like to start? The head?" He held the hammer over my head, and I flinched, squeezing my eyes shut tight. "Or the feet?" He moved the hammer slowly down my body and touched the cold iron to my toes.

I refused to open my eyes, terror gripping me as I continued my mantra. "This isn't real. This isn't real."

Gareth chuckled. "Feet it is."

The hammer came down, and I screamed.

I kept blacking out as they crushed every bone in my legs. My screams and pleas for mercy went unheeded, and I couldn't summon any more tears to cry. An illusion couldn't hurt this much. All the brain fog had lifted, and I was acutely aware of everything, including every excruciating moment since that first hammer blow.

They'd moved me to a worktable and were about to carve into my legs to remove the pulped bones when an overwhelming pressure began leaching into the cavern, like we were moving deeper and deeper underwater. The air crackled, and I vaguely registered Gareth and Hephaestus scrambling frantically, shouting at each other before the ceiling cracked open and light burst through.

I turned my head numbly, exhausted. A figure materialized out of the light, wings splayed, body rippling with power. He batted Gareth and the smith god aside like they were nothing.

The figure glided over to me, and I didn't have the energy to panic when I realized who it was. All I could do was lay there, not caring what happened to me next, as Bel scooped me up and lifted me into the sky.

I awoke, surrounded by a fluffy duvet, safe and warm in my bed. The sun filtered through the blinds and the open window let in a soft breeze, making the room the perfect temperature for sleep. I snuggled deeper into the covers.

The bedroom door opened, and I glanced up to see Bel coming through with two mugs of coffee. Against the wall, I glimpsed a dark, robed figure staring at me from the shadows, eyes gleaming. Then the door swung all the way open, and it was gone.

I started and scrambled up in bed, throwing off the covers and falling backward off the mattress.

Bel only stood there, not moving, a patient smile on his face. I looked at my legs, running my hands up and down, checking for injury. There was nothing, no evidence at all that they'd been hammered to a pulp.

Shaking, I looked up at Bel, who slowly set the mugs down on the beside table and sat. "I suppose I have a lot of things to explain."

"How did I get here? What's going on? How are my legs healed?"

Bel smiled sadly. "Meg, I know a lot has happened." His words were soft and measured. "Please know that you are safe."

"Not from you," I spat, raising my knees into my chest as I huddled in the corner.

"I'm not going to try to convince you of anything. Your mind has been played with more than you know, and you'll need plenty of time to recuperate and decide for yourself what's real." He shook his head and tears glistened in his eyes. "I'm so sorry I couldn't protect you."

When I said nothing, Bel took a deep breath and stood. "When you're ready to talk, come downstairs. I'll do my best to explain."

I observed the space behind the door as he closed it behind him, but no shadowy figures were hiding there this time. Once my body stopped shaking, I got to my feet and picked up the coffee mug he'd left behind. As much as I wanted that comforting hit of caffeine, I didn't trust it, so I clasped the mug between my hands and let the warmth seep into me.

When I entered the living room an hour later, Bel was sitting on the couch, cross-legged, his eyes staring into space. I'd been standing there for almost thirty seconds when he finally blinked and focused on me.

He smiled and his posture relaxed as he held out his hand to me. "I'm glad you came."

I skirted the room and stood as far from him as I could, comforted by the coffee table and large sofa in between us. He let his hand drop, but his expression stayed amiable.

"Tell me what you've experienced so far."

I looked at him incredulously, staying silent.

He grimaced. "That's fair. I'll tell you what's happened from our perspective, and then maybe you'll feel more comfortable?"

I leaned against the wall and crossed my arms over my chest.

He nodded. "Okay." He ran a hand through his hair and smoothed his beard in a few quick strokes. "This all started when you located Arthur."

My heart thudded painfully.

"When you returned home, you weren't alone. The Titans found a way to attach to you. I started noticing a change in your behavior. That incident with the mind erasing—"

"Incident?" I asked.

"I was trying to figure out what was going on and I got carried away," he said calmly. "But then you went and tracked down all the remaining links at once. That tipped the scales and you started to deteriorate mentally. The Titans had a firm hold on you. You began to talk about—" Bel searched for words "—a camp? You had conversations with people that weren't there. None of us could reach you. Your body was here, but your mind was somewhere else."

"I don't believe you."

Bel bowed his head. "I don't expect you to. Like I said, you'll have to determine it for yourself."

"I also remember you torturing me for weeks. Was that all an illusion, too?"

Bel took in a shuddering breath, looking pained... and guilty. "That was real, but it wasn't torture."

I raised my eyebrows in invitation for whatever ridiculous story he was about to tell me.

"We were doing an exorcism."

I faltered. Exorcism?

"We tried all kinds of techniques. Physical pain was the only thing that seemed to break through the illusions for a time. It got brutal, but I was getting desperate. I never meant for it to go that far, but... I couldn't let the Titans win."

Bel's gaze shifted again, and his mind was somewhere else. I didn't see his chest rising or falling with breath the entire time he sat, staring. Then he blinked and continued.

"Risha thought she'd found a solution, and I wasn't thinking. I was so overwhelmed and relieved, I didn't secure you properly. When I found the room empty—"

"The torture chamber," I clarified.

Bel looked at me. "What do you remember from that time?"

I relayed my experience, and he shook his head. "Let's drive to the lodge. I'll show you the room, prove it wasn't like that."

I chewed my lip.

Bel held up his hands. "Or you can head there yourself." He took out a key ring and picked out a specific key. "This will unlock the doors. Go see for yourself."

The trip to the lodge was uneventful, other than the sick feeling in my stomach. What if that room was different? What if I had been imagining most of what happened? Shame and guilt dominated me as I drove up the driveway to the lodge.

All was quiet, and when I entered, I crept down the stairs to the first door, unlocked it, and entered the subbasement. My hands trembled so badly I couldn't get the key in the lock. Once I managed it, my hand froze on the doorknob.

I had to know, but I didn't want to. What I'd felt with Gareth was so *real*. Giving that up would break me. I'd thought I'd found a home in him. I'd wanted so badly to believe it was true.

Just open it.

My hand twisted the knob and pushed the door inward. A sob tore from my throat as I flicked on the light.

A clean hospital bed. Medical equipment. An antiseptic smell. Evidence of magickal rituals and a few tools, including the extricator, but they were coated with healing magick. It thrummed off them with a palpable aura. These weren't tools for torture. The small shaft of light that had kept me company from the ventilation duct was gone too, and there was no evidence that anything had ever been there.

I searched through cupboards and drawers but found more of the same. I turned to the other doors in the subbasement corridor and checked those too, but it was all storage.

No chains, blades, crusted blood, or the smell of unwashed bodies and fear.

My stomach rolled, and I bolted up the stairs, racing outside. I barely made it off the porch before I fell to my knees and vomited. I purged everything until it was nothing but bile and then I continued to dry heave, tears streaming down my face.

I heard a car coming up the drive and spared a glance. Bel's car lurched to a stop, and the door popped open. He rushed to me as I stood on unsteady feet, letting him wrap me in his arms. He crushed me to him and whispered, "I'm so sorry," and "It's going to be okay."

He led me into the lodge to get me some water, wrapping my fingers around the glass and helping me lift it to my lips.

Once we'd settled on the couch, Bel continued his story. "When I found you were gone, I panicked. I knew they'd gotten you and I went off the last piece of information you'd given me before you retreated into yourself. My first inclination was to go after Gareth. Of course, I remembered him from the wars. He was a brutal general and had a cruel streak like you've never seen, but he hid it all behind charm and a smile. A true sociopath. He fit right in with the rest of the Titans' Six. With Risha's help, the minute I'd gathered enough energy, I went after you."

"But we'd already gone," I said, voice small. I was reeling, struggling to wrap my head around it. Something still seemed off.

"It took me some time to gather my strength again, but Ursal traced you to Lemnos."

"Lemnos?" I asked.

Bel nodded. "As soon as I could, I found Hephaestus's lair and pulled you out." He growled. "I know many Ætherim are on the Titan's side," he said with a disgusted sneer, "but I'd always thought Hephaestus was a friend."

"What happened to them?" I asked, almost afraid of the answer.

"I don't know. I didn't have enough power left to fight one of my own and still be guaranteed to get you out, so I left them there. Risha and Ursal did the lion's share of the work healing you."

But still, that sense of unease nagged at me. "Aren't there other legends of Lemnos?" I asked.

"I'm sure there are. You can't throw a stick in the Aegean without hitting a myth of some kind."

My mind was sifting through all the legends I knew. A sudden tiredness pulled at me, and I yawned.

"You should get some rest. We have some big decisions to make tomorrow."

I nodded. "I will. But wasn't there something about—"
Bel raised his eyebrows. "About…"
The fog took over and my brain felt fuzzy, bogged down.

"Come on, let's get you to bed," said Bel, holding out his hand to help me off the couch.

"Lemnos..." I muttered. "It was where... it was where..." I fought the confusion and kept digging through memories. A thought started to form and then blinding pain tore through my head.

"Meg, what's wrong?" asked Bel.

My vision blurred, wavering like static on an old tube TV.

"Illusion." Another blinding pain. From the corner of my eye, the cloaked figure appeared again, coming closer every time I blinked.

# Chapter Three

## Gareth

"**M**eg!" I bellowed, straining against my bindings to get to her. She was screaming as Bel flayed her alive, staring at me with eyes full of pain and fear, blaming me for not saving her.

Every time I struggled, the binds only got tighter, cutting into my skin. I couldn't breathe, but I wouldn't stop. The underworld pulsed around us with its eerie light, the massive gates of Tartarus before us. I heard the Titans crying out in despair, desperate and beating against the doors, trying to save their daughter and just as helpless.

In the shadows of the antechamber, my five broth ers-in-arms were equally bound, most of them dead, having succumbed to their struggles against the magickal restraints. Bel had us all. It was over. We'd failed.

The chamber shook as Bel's magick reached its peak. I watched helplessly as Meg's life drained out of her, drawn into the gates of Tartarus and sealing them shut forever.

The violet irises of her eyes dimmed before closing for the last time. Her face was covered in blood, the only part of her that Belsioch hadn't mutilated.

He turned to me, picking up Meg's body and throwing her at my feet, where she landed with a heavy squelching sound. The howl of agony that tore from my throat reverberated in the hollow, deafening. I crashed to the ground and inched toward her, crawling as best I could. She was gone, but I had to be near her, had to feel her next to me one last time.

"How sweet," sneered Belsioch. "Your devotion is touching." He motioned around at my dead brothers. Felix was breathing, but not for much longer. "You lose. I win." He chuckled. "But at least you died together."

The Titans beat against the gates so fiercely, bits of rock flaked and fell from the metal frame holding it tightly in place. Their heartbroken cries rose above Belsioch's cackles. All of it was for nothing.

I lowered my face to Meg's and placed a kiss on her forehead before lying down next to her, whispering my apologies as my vision went black.

"Get your hands off her!" I screamed.

Meg was fighting for her life, battling an enraged Belsioch while I lay bound and useless against the wall. We'd come so far and all I could do was watch as Meg slowly tired in her battle. Belsioch was toying with her now, a cat with its prey. The spear in his hand gleamed with a cold light in the shaft of sun filtering from the ceiling into the underground chamber.

He pushed her and Meg fell, spinning onto her shoulder and landing hard with a cry of pain. A loud crack of bone snapping set my teeth on edge. Belsioch kicked her in the stomach and she sprawled onto her back. She crawled backward, and he stomped on her knee, holding her in place.

"Meg!"

She looked at me with fear and pain in her eyes, and no small amount of betrayal. I hadn't kept her safe. My one job above all else. I'd failed her.

A flash of metal and it was over. Belsioch drove the spear into Meg's chest, the blade piercing her heart and pinning her to the rock beneath her. I watched in horror as the life left her body, fueling Belsioch's magick and glowing with an ominous purple-black light, an ethereal bruise that rose and disappeared.

I roared in anguish, breaking free of my bindings with a hard snap and charged at Belsioch, but he was ready for me. A long knife I hadn't even noticed appeared in his hand, and as I lunged, I barely felt the razor-sharp blade pierce my heart as it drove up through my sternum.

Belsioch let me drop, and I crawled toward Meg. At least we could be together at the end. My eyes closed, and I waited for death.

"Look out!" I warned, lunging to grab Meg out of the way of the sword crashing down toward her. The nephilim that bore it stepped around the corner and thrust the blade forward, spearing Meg and me through.

"Meg, no!" I cried, running forward. I'd been too late. I gathered her in my arms and cradled her to my chest. Her hand reached up and, with what strength she had left, she pulled my head down to speak into my ear. Her warm breath brushed over me as she whispered one word. "Illusion."

I looked at her quizzically, but before I could ask her what she meant, a sharp pain stabbed through me, and everything went black.

"Dream," said Meg, before a strange shadow morphed into a cloaked figure and stepped forward, grabbing Meg around the neck and breaking her spine in a movement so swift I had no time to react. Another figure lurched into view, tall and lithe. His hand closed over my eyes and my mind went dark.

*Lemnos.* The whisper came from the inky blackness that surrounded me. I was barely conscious as I floated in the empty space. *Lemnos.* The voice whispered again.

"Meg?" I croaked. My voice sounded flat and close, like I was in a small space.

*Fight. You have to fight!*

A crackling light appeared and pain lanced through my head, adding a brilliant network of stars piercing through the darkness.

Fire wreathed the room and I saw the same tall figure that had passed a hand over my face standing a foot away, next to the cloaked man. They were both pale and hard looking, their features sharp. The cloaked figure was older and by the resemblance, I could tell they were related. He stared at me with a twisted grin as Meg writhed in pain at their feet.

I recognized them. I'd met them before, on the field of battle. Their magick could cut down swaths of people at a time, locking them in nightmarish sleep. Hypnos and Morpheus.

The grin on Hypnos's face wavered as he saw the look of recognition dawn. The world around me shuddered and Hypnos strode forward, hand outstretched. I could feel the pull of sleep dragging me down again.

I had to get to Meg. But what if this was still just a dream?

I flexed my hand and my claws burst forward. With a snarl, I drove a claw into my thigh. My mind cleared and the picture in front of me snapped back into focus.

Hypnos moved faster and his magick swirled around me. I swiped at him, leaping to my feet. Morpheus looked around in alarm.

"Don't lose your focus on the girl!" Hypnos snapped at his son. Morpheus turned back to Meg, face pinched in concentration. I charged at Hypnos, shifting into my wolf form in midair and knocking him off his feet. Speed was my only advantage, and before he could defend himself, I tore his throat out. It wouldn't kill him, but it would slow him down and hopefully give us a few minutes head start.

Morpheus abandoned Meg and faced me, the nightmares curling around his fingers as he considered me with cold indifference. I shifted back to my human form.

"Without your father or brothers around to bolster your power, the nightmares wouldn't hold me for long. Let me take her and you can tend to your father."

"So noble," he spat.

I shrugged. "If you don't, I'll rip your throat out as well. You might not heal as well as he does, though."

Morpheus's face twitched as he fought the rage threatening to explode from him. "I'm just as powerful as him."

"You don't exist without him," I said plainly. "But he'll be just fine without you."

His pupils dilated until the irises were gone. The magick at his fingertips crackled and snaked around him, looking for a target. Inching toward Meg.

I took a step forward. "Let her be."

"Belsioch will be here soon, anyway. You have nowhere to run."

A chill stole through me. "So you're working for him?" Another step forward.

Morpheus sneered. "*With* him. We intercepted you."

"Seems like he's the only one that benefits. You do all the work and he waltzes in to finish the job."

His magick paused in its circuit around his hands and retreated just a fraction. I took another step, and I noticed Meg start to stir.

"You don't know anything," said Morpheus. His attempt at sounding confident failed.

Meg made a small noise and in the split second that Morpheus glanced away from me, I lashed out and shredded his throat. He clutched at it and fell. Before he even hit the ground, I had Meg in my arms and took off running.

We were in a cave, but I could hear the crashing of waves not that far away. I ran toward the sound, straining my eyes in the darkness. My foot caught an uneven part of the rocky tunnel floor and I went sprawling, tucking myself around Meg and protecting her head as I rolled. My back hit the stone wall and knocked the wind out of me.

"Are you okay?" Meg's voice was tired, and she pushed against me weakly. "Let me up."

I released her as I tried to catch my breath. She glanced at me nervously, inching away before patting herself down and running her hands over her legs, bending them gingerly. She sighed in relief.

"What did you dream?" I asked her.

She looked at me for a long moment and I could feel the distrust through our bond. That hurt more than any physical pain.

"That *you* pulverized every bone in my legs to fashion the key for the gates of Tartarus. And Bel saved me. I know the part about him being the good guy was a trick, but..."

I nodded, chest tight. "You're questioning my motives. It felt too real."

Tears appeared in her eyes and I reached for her, but she shied away. "Please, Meg. Don't shut me out. This is what Hypnos and his sons do. I've seen plenty of my brothers fall to his illusions and never make their way back out. Talk to me."

She was shaking in the chill of the cave. "You set me up. *You* handed me to the enemy."

I didn't think my anger at Belsioch could burn any fiercer, but it did now. I pushed it down and spoke gently, imploring. "Do you know what they made me dream?"

She shook her head. Her emotions roiled, wanting me to alleviate her fears but stuck in the horror that those nightmares caused.

"They made me watch you die, a hundred different ways. And I couldn't save you. Over and over again—" my voice broke "—I watched the life leave your eyes, and all I could do was hope my death would follow quickly."

She had to feel my earnestness through the bond, the truth in my words. Tears were falling down her face freely now and she nodded, hesitant, before diving into my chest and clutching me tight.

My arms wrapped around her and relief flooded through me. I lifted my eyes to the ceiling and said a silent word of thanks to the Fates for saving our hides yet again.

The lingering sleep magick clung to me, lulling me back down now that it had a moment of rest to work on me.

"Gareth?" Meg's hand touched my face, and I raised my own to cover hers. My eyes were so heavy. I could only grumble a response.

She blew out a frustrated breath. "Sorry in advance."

Before I could ask what for, a hard slap to the face brought me back around. I shook my head and rubbed my face. "You really pack a punch."

"Do you need another?" There was a smile in her voice.

"I'm awake," I said, getting to my feet.

I moved to sweep her back up in my arms, but she protested. "I'm fine. I could use the run."

"Are you sure? I promise, no more surprise barrel rolls."

She took my hand and smiled. "I trust you to lead."

I took off, pulling her behind me, and within a few more minutes we could see light up ahead. The wild ocean met us when we broke out onto the sandy shore. We must've been on the other side of the island. The tide was coming in and our feet splashed into warm water just a foot from the mouth of the cave.

"Do you think you can transport us?" I asked.

She concentrated and the swells of time moved around her, but only slightly. Her violet eyes shot to me with panic. "Not yet. How long before they wake up?"

In response to her question, the ground beneath our feet shook and rubble crashed down from the roof of the cave.

I felt her pulse quicken and took her other hand. "Just relax and concentrate."

"Relax? There are angry Ætherim bearing down on us!"

Through our bond, I poured every ounce of calm I had, while boosting her power with my own. Her eyes widened as she realized what I was doing. "How about now?"

Meg smiled. Time rushed around us with force, and we were off.

# Meg

The murmur of pilgrims gathered outside the temple was a soft susurrus of noise that blended with the breeze in the laurel trees. The sun was hot as it beat down on the stone arcade leading to the temple gates and wisps of cloud skated cheerily across a sky, giving way to twilight.

"Are we in Delphi?" asked Gareth.

I nodded and pulled him farther away as we got more curious looks from the passersby heading toward the temple. Pilgrims from all over the known world found their way to Apollo's temple at Delphi, but even so, Gareth's tartan drew stares. Or maybe it was something to do with the fact that he looked like Heracles reborn.

"Looks a bit different. When I was here last it was a shadow of what it is now." He was gazing around him in amazement. "It's incredible." His eyes took on a keen interest. "Who are we going to find here?"

I shook my head. "I'm not sure. Now that I'm trying to find a signature, I've got nothing. I might have undershot it."

The marble of the temple gleamed and I could just see the blue-gray stone lining the floor of the cella, where many travelers crowded to wait to hear from the Pythia.

"I might have waylaid you, just a bit."

Gareth and I both turned in surprise. The voice had come out of nowhere, right next to us. A man with dark olive skin and large brown eyes that shone with keen intelligence appraised us, a casual grin on his face. He was taller than me, but less than average height. Even so, his lean frame was corded with muscle and everything about him said *speed*.

Then I noticed the sandals he wore, with an image of wings pressed into the leather. And the smallest tattoo in the hollow of his throat of a caduceus.

"Lord Hermes?" I asked.

He inclined his head. "Guilty." His grin became toothy. "Hopefully Hypnos didn't cause you too much trouble."

Gareth stepped forward and slightly in front of me. Not directly challenging the god before us, but making it clear he wasn't going to tolerate whatever plans were brewing.

"Simmer down, wolf. I don't mean you any harm. Belsioch's minions were going to intercept you again, so I cut them off before they could."

My mouth fell open in shock and with my new wolfish instincts, my claws started to erupt from my fingertips with a knee-jerk reaction to my anxiety.

Hermes chuckled. "That's an interesting accessory. I don't think that was part of the original design?"

I blinked rapidly and stared at my hand, willing the claws away.

The mischievous god lived up to his name with a grin that promised all sorts of trouble. "Secret's safe with me. And don't look so surprised about my intercession. There are more of us that hate Belsioch than you might think."

My mind was spinning, trying to figure out how we were even talking to Hermes. "I didn't think Ætherim had the ability to time travel?"

Also read: should I be worried about that?

"I don't." Hermes flicked his wrist to resettle his sleeve. "But most of us can travel back and forth if we have a deep connection to a place. We can slide into past versions of ourselves. Time's a funny thing when you live forever."

A chill stole over me. "I wasn't aware that was possible."

The god waggled his eyebrows. "Lucky for you Belsioch wasn't around here much. Can't say the same for some of the other places you're going to have to visit."

"Isn't this Apollo's temple?" asked Gareth.

Hermes turned curious eyes on him, and I could feel my mate's unease. "We have had our disagreements, but I've always been close with my half brother."

I tried to change the subject. "So you're against Bel. Does that mean you're pro-Titan?"

Hermes leaned against a pillar and crossed his legs at the ankles. "I wouldn't say 'pro'. More like 'the enemy of my enemy'..." He waved his hand in wide loops to finish the sentence. "Belsioch has been a thorn in my balls for a long time. He's starting to push his way into every pantheon's business and self-elect his ass as the god of gods. As if we didn't already have enough to deal with, with Zeus's ego."

Anger flashed across his face before he quickly covered it up with another amicable smile. "But if helping you makes trouble for him, then I'm all for it." Hermes's eyes shifted out of focus and back again. "Not sure how much longer you'll be hidden here though. He's looking for you."

"Let's go," said Gareth, voice hitching with anxiety.

"Oh, I wouldn't do that, either," said Hermes. "He'll just divert you again."

I could feel a flash of anger coming through the bond and it took me a moment to realize it wasn't my own emotion. I reached out and grabbed Gareth's hand, stroking the back of it with my thumb. "Any suggestions?" I asked Hermes.

"I'd say go visit the Oracle, hang out for a while. When Belsioch finds you... he might find himself with a bigger problem to contend with."

"What should we do going forward? If he can waylay us at any time, how can we travel without getting trapped?"

"As long as he has a lock on you, he can. But if you occlude your signature, you'll stay hidden. Also something the Oracle can help you with." He winked. "Oh, and one more thing."

There was a rush of breeze and my skin tingled. A glance down showed my clothing had switched out to classical era Greek attire, the soft white linen billowing against my skin and exciting gooseflesh. Gareth's tartan had also changed, but his outfit was flashing a decidedly greater amount of thigh.

"Now you won't draw undue attention," said Hermes. "Although that'll mean fuck all when Belsioch shows up." He pointed his thumb toward the temple proper in a firm motion and spoke with a lazy southern drawl. "Go on, get."

I snorted a laugh. He'd clearly taken to modern-era speech, and while it was crazy to hear it in this setting, I didn't hate it. "Thank you."

"Don't thank me yet."

Hermes disappeared without a sound or a puff of smoke, no evidence that anyone had even been there.

Still holding tight to Gareth's hand, we walked quickly toward the cella. The other pilgrims gave us a wide berth, and I heard plenty of whispers and felt the stares.

Knowing my thoughts, Gareth leaned down and spoke into my ear. "I'm not the only one they're looking at. You could stand among the goddesses and not look out of place."

I looked into his eyes, and for just that brief instant, I forgot about the trouble that was heading our way. Apollo's priests standing at the altar were watching us with keen appraisal through the haze of pine and laurel incense wafting around them.

As we stepped through the temple entrance, the air shifted. Closer and warmer, the musk of bodies packed together around us more pronounced. As we joined the queue to the Pythia's cave, one of the priests pulled us aside.

"Follow me."

Gareth and I exchanged a quick glance and fell into step behind him. He was wearing distinctive, embroidered robes and kept his head high as he brushed past the line of pilgrims with us close behind. People didn't protest, only stared after us curiously, sharing furtive whispers in our wake.

The air became damp with a scent of something acidic underpinning it that I couldn't place. The drip of water became a steady trickle the farther down we walked, the steps worn smooth after so many hundreds of years. The temple's exterior may have changed many times, but this cave remained untouched. Neither of us was keen on going underground after what we'd just escaped, but at least this one was full of people.

My eyes adjusted to the darkness and shapes began to emerge from the shadowy corners where the brazier light didn't reach. Eyes shining in the gloom belonged to ghosts, standing in silence as they waited, most of them long dead. I didn't want to think too much about what they'd done to find themselves bound to this place.

There were etchings on the walls, ornamentation carved into archways, all of it fading with age. There was a broken mosaic pattern in seemingly random patches on the floor, either worn away or broken apart on purpose.

I gazed ahead at the woman in long robes, a veil over her face, as she sat on the tripod seat at the end of the promenade. She was looking up through heavy eyelids, half out of focus as she swayed slightly back and forth. This was the oracle of legend, the Pythia, the voice of the gods that saw the future and delivered fates.

"You're not the visitors I was expecting next," she said, her voice a harsh rasp that clawed its way from her throat. A sharp glare broke through her drug-induced haze, and I was pinned to the spot. There was nothing much intimidating about this woman, but when she looked at you like new prey walking into her lair, you knew she meant it.

"Lord Hermes gave them favor," said the priest, hesitating.

The Pythia straightened and drew back her veil. Her face was gaunt, with hollowed cheeks. Her teeth were stark white against dark bronze skin with razor-sharp incisors too long to belong to a human, but without the characteristic taper of vampire teeth.

Her eyes pinned us to the spot as she fixed her full attention on us, the irises glowing with a preternatural flash before the light faded. "Hermes," she hissed. "And what does he want from you?"

"Nothing. We have a common enemy and he offered to help."

"The gods don't make offers without receiving something of greater value from you," the Pythia scoffed.

"If the enemy is big enough, they do," said Gareth, his tone warning her not to overstep.

The Pythia's head tilted to the side and a lazy grin swept across her face. "Aren't you just the perfect protector?" Her eyes flicked to me and back to him. "And what lengths would you go to, to keep her from harm?"

Without hesitation, Gareth said, "I'd go to the ends of the earth."

A hoarse, dry noise that might've been a laugh croaked out of her. Spindly fingers grasped her knees as she leaned in, a ghoulish, haunted look on her face. "You'll be held to it before this is over."

The Pythia drew her veil back down and motioned to the priest. "Take an offering from each of them."

Gareth immediately stepped in front of me and this time there was no question that the woman in the high seat was laughing at us. The cackle sent chills racing across my skin, anxiety pooling in my gut.

"Stand down. I need blood from the both of you if you want me to help you hide from Belsioch."

The priest drew forward again with a small pen knife bared at the ready.

"It's just a little prick," she said, her cackle redoubling.

I nodded at Gareth, and we both held our hands out. The priest swiped the blade across the meaty part of our palms, taking a piece of linen from a pouch at his side and dabbing the wounds with it, working fast to beat our healing abilities.

By the time he'd brought the scrap of fabric to the Pythia, our skin had knit back together. The woman slid from her seat, her toes pointing as they reached for solid ground. Her skirts pooled and swept around her feet as she glided toward the darkest corner of the chamber. The shadows shifted and the air pressure in the room changed. She'd opened a door.

The priest motioned for us to follow. The air was much thicker in this part of the chamber, the gasses boiling up from cracks in the floor settling thickly. My head was starting to swim and everything took on a rainbow afterglow. Gareth had the height advantage, so he wasn't exposed to as much vapor.

The door she'd opened was cut into the stone. I could tell just by looking that when it was closed, it would sit seamlessly in the rocky wall and be undetectable to anyone who didn't already know it was there. A greenish light emanated from the brazier in this room, the eerie effect putting me on edge.

The Pythia had the linen scraps laid out on a table and was gathering herbs and potions from jars along shelves cut into the rock. Her fingertips were stained with a dark, inky color that was crusted into her sharpened nails.

She splashed a harsh-smelling liquid on our bloody offerings and laid herbs in the center before rolling them up tight. Suddenly, she stilled, looking off into space with a hawkish glare.

Then I realized what caught her attention. That same humming sound and the pressure of someone forcing their way through time was building around us.

"Bel found us," I gasped. My body immediately tried to shift, but Gareth reversed the impulse through the bond.

"We can't give away our secrets yet." He attempted a reassuring smile, but it didn't reach eyes pinched with worry.

The Pythia, undeterred, marched back into the main chamber with the bundle, speaking words under her breath. From the words I caught, it was an incantation of concealment.

Her magick churned, and as her spell built, Bel forced his way through faster, already aware of the magick working against him. A horrible screeching sound rent the air and a portal opened.

Bel stepped through it with a confident, dark smile on his face.

"Got you."

# CHAPTER FIVE

# Gareth

A snarl ripped from me, and I readied to launch myself at Belsioch.

Two things happened simultaneously. The Pythia spat and threw the bundle into the fire, and Belsioch thrust his hand outward and hit us with binding magick that took us both down.

The Pythia shrieked in anger and backed away, the priest nowhere to be seen. "You dare force your way into Apollo's sanctum!"

Belsioch sneered at her. "This isn't your concern, harpy."

"I'm not the one you should be worried about." She was staring at him, mouth open like a cat scenting the air, fangs dripping with saliva. "My lord will not be pleased with this transgression."

A flicker of worry flashed across Belsioch's face. "Then we'll be on our way."

A strong wind built as the god wove magick around us, preparing to transport us back with him. I struggled against the binding and it started to weaken. I just needed more time.

Meg's eyes were wide as she silently stared at the man that had caused her so much torment. Rage boiled within me, and the bindings fractured farther.

"Meg, can you slow him down?" I asked.

She blinked and looked at me, uncomprehending. "What?"

"Can you close the portal? It's time magick, right?"

She startled and nodded. "Yeah, maybe I can."

Meg's magick blazed and Belsioch roared. "Don't try to fight me! It will only make your punishment worse." He poured more of his own power into his attempts at transporting us, but he underestimated just what it would take to move three people instead of just himself.

I could feel her fear, but she didn't back down. Her magick reached for the portal and, in a blink, it disappeared.

Belsioch whipped around and stared, furious. I almost had the binding broken as he marched over to Meg and hauled her up by her hair. "You stupid girl!"

My binding snapped, and I lunged at him as a golden arrow flew so close by my head that the wind moved my hair. It struck Belsioch through the shoulder and he dropped Meg into my waiting arms. I sprinted across the chamber to stand with the fierce golden god whose bow was leveled at Belsioch with another arrow nocked. Anger radiated from him, the air around him moving like waves of heat.

Meg gently patted me on the shoulder, and I realized I was still carrying her in my arms. Reluctantly, I set her on her feet.

When Apollo spoke, his warm, rumbling baritone shook with fury. "That was your only warning. Leave my temple, or die."

Only Ætherim can kill others of their kind, so this wasn't an idle threat.

"You wouldn't dare," said Belsioch. But as he stood there, grasping the arrow in his shoulder, he didn't seem so sure.

"You trespassed. No one would look twice if I cut you down." Apollo's aim was rock steady. He stood a head taller than me, and he had a quiver full of arrows strapped across broad shoulders that left no doubt as to the force behind each pull of the bowstring.

Belsioch set to work calling the portal back up and Apollo waited, not taking his eyes off his target.

The portal was steadily growing in size. At about halfway, Belsioch turned and grinned, crossing his arms. "On second thought," he sneered, "I don't think you have the guts."

Apollo's reaction was immediate. He loosed the arrow.

But Belsioch was ahead of him.

Too late I realized magick had been wrapping around my chest and with an almost imperceptible movement of Belsioch's fingers, I jerked and spun forward just before the arrow left the bowstring, putting me right in its path.

Meg screamed as the shaft punched through my chest, the force of it sending me flying across the room. Out of the corner of my eye, I saw the coward jump through the portal and flee.

I landed on my side and all the air *whooshed* out of my lungs. Meg tripped and slid across the floor in her haste and scrambled to me. The arrow protruded out of my back and my entire body burned with pain. Her face blurred in my vision and my attempt to reach for her failed.

"Gareth?" She looked above her to where Apollo must've been standing. "What do I do?" she asked, panicked.

Apollo knelt down and examined me, his fingers pressing around the exit wound.

"That son of a bitch," he cursed. "I don't care where we meet next, I will end him."

Arms appeared in my field of vision and the arrow jostled as Apollo gripped it and snapped the end off. I bit back a cry of pain as he forced the shaft through the wound tract and pulled it out the other side.

"I'll do my best to heal him, but—"

"That's my specialty." I recognized Hermes's voice and the god moved into view, his face grim. "What have you done, brother?"

"Don't start," Apollo sniffed. "Belsioch used him as a shield."

"So he's gone full coward, then," said Hermes. He leaned down and rolled me onto my back. A paralyzing sensation spread through my body, and I couldn't speak.

"Unfortunately, since my brother's bow is made to kill rogue gods and other big, nasty things, it's full of magick that you can't tolerate," Hermes explained, humming thoughtfully as he poked around at the wound. I could feel some other power at work, but it was barely cutting through the pain and numbness.

"What does that mean?" asked Meg.

"It'll act like a poison to his system." He picked up the arrow remnant and examined it. "Good gods, you really loaded for bear."

"I didn't come here planning to tickle him to death. I'm not Eros."

Hermes snorted a laugh but sobered at the look of disbelief Meg shot him. "Apologies. My bedside manner is lacking."

The Pythia handed Hermes a vial of something viscous. "This might help."

Hermes uncorked the vial and recoiled. "Shit, what the hell did you just hand me?"

"Special concoction," said the Pythia. I could hear a grin in her voice.

Hermes widened his eyes in exasperation and shook his head. "Special." He looked at Meg. "I've got a better idea." He moved aside. "Let the construct do the work."

"Excuse me?" said Meg, her worry over me giving way to anger at being referred to that way.

Hermes stared back at her calmly. "Sore subject?" He waved his hand. "No matter. Use your magick on him."

She shook her head in confusion. "I don't have healing magick."

"Kid, you've got the kind of magick that can solve any problem." He looked at her pointedly.

"I'm not following."

Hermes blew out a breath. "Don't make me make him sing the immortal words of Cher." He pointed at Apollo, who raised an eyebrow.

"No," he said, flatly.

Meg was twisting her hands in her lap, and I longed to reach for them, but couldn't move. "I understand what you're saying, but I can't just turn back time. Time would have to reconcile the injury, he'd wind up getting hurt another way. What's done is done."

"Then make the magick a little more localized," said Hermes.

Meg's patience ran out. "Can you please just get to the point?"

If Hermes was offended by her temper, he didn't show it. "Okay. I'm giving you some grace because you're stressed out right now." He pointed at my chest. "Weave your magick around the injury and turn back the clock. Just that part. Everything else stays the same, nothing is disrupted, nothing has to be rectified."

Meg took a deep breath and nodded. "I've never done that before, but it makes sense. If I lose control of it though, I could kill him."

Apollo spoke. "If you don't, he'll die anyway."

Meg shot him a glare and mumbled something under her breath, but continued. Warily, she placed her hands on my chest. I wanted to give her an approving nod or some kind of reassurance, but my body was fully paralyzed.

At first, nothing happened. I could tell she was struggling to concentrate. She looked up at the two gods and the oracle crowding around her. "Can you give me a little space, please?"

They backed away, Hermes looking entertained. Even Apollo's mouth twitched into a grin.

Meg laid her hands on my chest and closed her eyes, breathing deep. Then her magick began to work itself into my body. It was just a dull sensation to start, then it coalesced around the wound. The numbness in my body began to recede, but that only meant I could feel the pain again. Her brow knit as she felt my discomfort, but she pushed it aside and focused.

I stared at her in amazement. She had started to glow with an ethereal light that emanated from within, her skin illuminated. The magick was focused solely on the wound tract now, and the pain ebbed as the hole began to close. My whole body felt like I'd been hit by lightning.

"It's working," she breathed.

I almost had all of my senses returned to me when a sharp pain jolted through me with a shock. I gasped and Meg startled. "What was that?" she asked Hermes.

He leaned forward. "You need to detach from him. Pull your magick back, it's starting to break away from your control."

Another jolt shot through me and the world around me wavered.

"Pull it back," Hermes said, a little sharper this time.

"I'm trying," Meg said. "It's not working."

The world fell out from under me. My stomach dropped as I plummeted into empty space, everything turning dark. I heard Meg scream my name and then there was silence.

# CHAPTER SIX

# Meg

I watched with horror as Gareth flashed away into time, and I couldn't do anything to stop it. The empty patch of floor stained with his blood was all that was left.

"What happened?" asked Apollo.

Hermes laid a hand on my shoulder. "I'm sure he's fine. It was just a little wormhole. He's healed, so there's that."

Apollo made a thoughtful noise. "He's lost in time somewhere?"

I nodded, numb, searching my mind for the best option to bring him home. "I have to go into a trance to find him."

"I don't think you'll be able to go anywhere, even if you did figure out where he is," said Hermes. "Try to tap the time stream."

He was being ridiculous, but I reached for the current just to prove him wrong. Nothing. "Fuck! Not again!" I looked at Hermes accusingly. "What did you do?"

Hermes held up his hands. "I didn't do anything."

"Did Bel figure out how to block me?" I'd been stuck before, when I went searching for Gareth the first time, but Bel wouldn't have had any reason to block me then.

Hermes shook his head. "I think it was your old man."

I instantly soured. "He's not my father, for one. For another, why and how would he have?"

"We're not so helpless as we allow Belsioch to believe." The raspy voice was deeper than how the Pythia normally sounded. I turned to find her sitting on her tripod chair, veil hanging over her face as she breathed in the noxious gasses seeping through the fissures at her feet.

Apollo strode forward, his golden sandals soundless as he moved. "Kronos?"

My whole body spasmed as fear gripped me. I'd never spoken to any of them, never seen them. Only heard stories, none of which were flattering. I've only ever hated them, knowing why they created me and refusing to play their game. It was easy to hate someone you didn't know.

Hermes helped me to my feet and stood behind me as we approached the Pythia, but I got the feeling it was less for support and more to make sure that I didn't bolt. Not that I would've had the chance of outrunning either of the gods. Hell, the Pythia was wiry, but she probably wasn't a slouch either.

Slowly, her head lifted, and the Pythia's eyes, irises glowing like the iridescence of fireflies, fixed on me. A ghost of a smile played across her face and my chest filled with butterflies, heart hammering. That wasn't a cruel smile, and as she continued to watch me the smile grew into something glad, relieved.

"Megiste." That one word, spoken with... pride... had me taking another two steps forward, hands clasping nervously, knuckles white.

But I couldn't speak. My mind was racing too fast to hold on to any cohesive thought, let alone say it aloud.

"I am glad to see you at last," Kronos continued. "I've waited a hundred years for this moment." The Pythia's face twisted into a frown. "Unfortunately, we don't have much time. Belsioch is already planning his next strike."

"Are you the one that's keeping me here?" I asked. "Did you lock me out? And in Gareth's time, too?"

The Pythia's eyes shifted once I'd started speaking and I could see—as much as I was loath to admit it—the fatherly pride in the gaze.

"Yes. I needed to ensure that you couldn't leave without giving Gareth a chance. It cost me, but I was willing to take the risk. Same as now. You need to find Andrus. Gareth will be alright. Hyperion still has a few tricks up his sleeve. He'll keep your mate safe."

"How do I know it's the truth?" Even as the words left my mouth, I knew it was a knee-jerk question I regretted.

Kronos didn't seem to mind. "You know it is. Once you start trusting yourself, this journey will be much easier, for all of you. Never doubt what you already know."

The hatred I carried for the Titans welled up at that, wanted to spit back a retort, but I quashed it before it could. Kronos was studying me intently, and the gazes of the two gods were also on me, curious and appraising. "And if I continue this journey, where will it end?"

"Wherever you want it to."

I blinked and did a double take. "What?"

Kronos smiled sadly. "I will not deny that I have my hopes that you will find us. But I also cannot deny that I made mistakes, miscalculations, as Belsioch so kindly pointed out. You hate us, and I understand why."

The Pythia slid from her chair and stepped across the fissures, long, spindly legs making easy work of it. She stopped in front of me and reached out her hand, waited for me to take it. Her hands were dry and warm, and once my hand rested in hers, she closed both her hands over it.

"All I can do is ask your forgiveness, and tell you how sorry I am." She tilted her head to the side and a knowing glint sparked in her eye. "You'll also doubt the veracity of these words and will convince yourself it was a trick. I won't waste time trying to convince you otherwise. You have a mind of your own."

I inhaled sharply at that, and the Pythia's fingers tightened reassuringly.

"Use it well."

The Pythia collapsed, unconscious, and Apollo was there to catch her fall. He lifted her in his arms and carried her toward an antechamber, where I saw the priests waiting silently. He handed her over to their care and turned back to us.

"Do you know where you need to go next?" he asked. "The least I can do is make sure you arrive there safely."

I was still reeling from the encounter with Kronos, but I nodded. "Athens."

Apollo blanched. "Shit." He looked at Hermes, who sighed.

"Why is it that you always make offers before you know the details, and then rely on me to fulfill them?"

"How was I supposed to know that she'd say 'Athens'?"

Hermes gave him a droll stare. "You're the god of prophecy."

Apollo shrugged. "If I went around looking into the future all the time, it wouldn't be a surprise. This way it keeps things interesting."

"I take it you're fighting with Athena again?"

"She started it."

Hermes's jaw ticked as he contemplated his half brother. "Fine." He turned to me. "Let's go."

Apollo called after us as we climbed the stairs out of the chamber. "Good luck. And make sure your stay in the city is a short one."

As we walked out of the temple grounds, Hermes shook off his annoyance. I got the impression he was planning his revenge on Apollo, and I briefly wondered what kind of pranks the gods pulled on each other. Ha ha, I destroyed your temple? I got you good this time, I massacred your chosen acolytes? Have fun kickin' around this shadow realm I trapped you in for the next thousand years?

"The Pythia completed the ritual to ensure you and Gareth stay hidden from Belsioch. As you find the others it may get a bit tricky but at least he won't be breathing down your neck for a little while."

"Eventually we will run into him. He's not giving up that easily."

"Then you'll just have to get creative." He slapped me on the back. "Cheer up, you've already avoided or escaped him plenty of times."

"That's reassuring," I said flatly.

When I looked around me again, I realized we were in a completely different place. The city walls of what I assumed was Athens loomed ahead. I stopped in my tracks. "Wow."

Hermes nodded appreciatively. "It is quite something. I'll see you to the city gates, but I can't go farther. I'm not currently fighting with Athena, but she's never been a huge fan of mine."

I nodded. "Understood. I appreciate you getting me this far."

Hermes put his hands on his hips. "That's very nice, thank you. Nobody ever gives me the appreciation I deserve."

I resisted rolling my eyes. Once we were within easy walk of the gates, I turned to him. "Maybe I'll see you again?"

Hermes looked grim this time as he said, "I'm afraid we may not have a choice. This is going to get very messy, no matter how it ends."

On that positive note, I forged ahead to see what Athens had to offer.

I found out in short order why Apollo had advised me to hurry. My first impression of Athens was noise. A lot of chaos. People packed into the streets, preparing supplies, readying defenses. Villagers from the outlying areas crowded behind the walls, searching for a place to stay safe if the Persians made good on their threats as Xerxes stomped across the countryside.

How was I going to find anyone in this crush of people? Finding the general area would be easy enough, but pinpointing him with so much other activity going on would be next to impossible. There was no small gathering of Strangers here either, which made things more difficult.

Once I'd given myself a chance to acclimate to the situation, I found I could narrow my focus down. With the new enhancements I'd gained from Gareth—

If he were here right now, I'm sure he'd have a much better idea of what to do. But the faster I found Andrus, the sooner I could get Gareth back from whatever place in time I'd sent him to.

I filtered out the humans and an overwhelming number of ghosts lingering here and focused on the Strangers. If I kept my range within twenty feet of myself, I could hold the focus without something disrupting it. Now all I needed to do was comb a massive city full of panicked citizens to find my quarry.

To make matters worse, the sun was starting to set. I managed to find a quieter section of the street, to the side of an empty merchant stall that had closed up early. I could still smell the lingering spices and charred meat, with a hint of yeasted dough. My stomach growled, and I wished I could glamour rocks into money like the fae always did. I could also have used that money to buy a safe place to sleep, if there were any to be had.

I didn't know what kind of place this was after dark, but I was hesitant to find out without any kind of weapon on me.

But that wasn't quite accurate anymore, was it?

Reaching inward the way Gareth had taught me, I sought out my wolf. She answered with a tentative step forward and I could feel another consciousness overlaying my own, all the primal instincts she had melding seamlessly with me. When I didn't show any sign of resistance, she got a little bolder. My movement began to change, and I walked with a smoother gait as I moved farther back into the shadows, just in case I transformed without intending to.

People who passed by would elicit different instincts in me based on smell. Most were fearful and preoccupied, but every once in a while there would be a predator among them. Some human, some not. They would all have the same type of hot, acidic odor, and I could hear the blood rushing as they anticipated a fight or a struggle, having spotted their intended target.

A burly man with a shaved head and the wiry muscles of someone retired from a life of hard labor skulked into my zone. I got the impression of danger emanating from him and my wolf snarled, trying to lunge forward in my mind to take control.

"Not yet," I said out loud.

The man turned his head when he heard me speak and I noted a huge scar across his face. My wolf was just waiting for me to give the word. A grin twisted his face and a mouth full of jagged teeth turned my stomach.

"I don't want any trouble," I said, holding out my hands and taking a step back. Inwardly, I gave my wolf the green light.

The man took another step and reached out a hand already covered in scars and scuffs and dried blood. Then he stopped dead in his tracks as my nails elongated into claws.

"I don't want any trouble," I repeated.

The man nodded and scurried off.

I watched him disappear with a renewed sense of confidence, thanking my wolf as she settled back in my mind, but not so far away that she couldn't warn me of impending danger.

When you're used to relying on your ability to sense people, and that's taken away, you never realize what a daunting task it can be to locate someone otherwise. How do people do it? A needle in a stack of needles, that's what I was searching for. Only this was even more difficult because this particular needle could move around at will. There was nothing to stop him from moving to one sector of the city I'd already covered while I swept another.

It was well into the night, and I'd covered maybe a quarter of the city. The people had thinned out, most of them either bedding down for the night or sequestered in a tavern or brothel.

I needed to get off the street and find a place to rest. Or maybe go outside the city walls altogether. I'd probably be safer out there. High above me stood the Acropolis and the Propylaea, shining bright in the moonlight, the white marble of the massive gates still new and polished. Maybe I could seek refuge there.

Just don't mention Apollo, apparently.

The atmosphere shifted as I reached the road that led up to the outcrop. The stone walls cast harsh shadows across the cobbled brick street. This walk was much less harried than in the main part of the city. It was peaceful up here, high above everything else. As I grew close, I kept watch for acolytes or priests or anyone that might be a part of Athena's cult. I didn't want to trespass while looking for a night of sanctuary.

The gentle breeze pulled at my hair and the smell of salty sea air surrounded me, the waves crashing in the distance. I heard an owl call and paused to look for it, scanning the olive trees planted in the sandy soil that lined the path to the main entrance.

As I mounted the stairs, I trod lightly enough that my shoes only made a small *snick, snick* sound with each step.

It wasn't until I'd reached the pillars of the temple itself that I saw the first hints of people being present. The beautiful altar standing, full of offerings, had oil lamps burning and incense freshly lit. My enhanced hearing caught the soft scraping of footsteps within the temple, and I looked up to see a priestess coming toward me.

I couldn't tell how old she was. Her eyes were piercing green as they settled on me, carrying a weight in them that belied a more mature age. But instead of telling me to get lost, something like recognition dawned and a small smile creased her face.

"Welcome to the temple of Athena. May I ask what you are seeking?"

She spoke with the authority of a high-ranking priestess. I bowed my head in deference. "I was hoping to find a place to sleep safe tonight. I'd be happy just tucking into a corner outside."

She shook her head. "No need for that. Children of the Great Ones shouldn't be cast aside and left to fend for themselves."

# CHAPTER SEVEN

# Meg

I blinked as I realized what she'd said. "How—"

She waved me off and motioned for me to follow her further into the complex. "There is an aura shared among the powerful beings. Once you know what to look for, it is not difficult to pick it out."

The interior of the temple was warm, but not stifling. The heady aroma of incense was thick, and I gaped as Athena's massive statue came into view, made entirely of bronze and at least twenty feet tall. Mosaics were inlaid in the floor, not as detailed as the friezes, but you got the gist.

Most of the lamps were extinguished at this hour, but there was enough light to make our way through to the smaller chambers on the outskirts of the temple. The priestess motioned to a small room with a straw mattress, washbasin, and chamber pot.

"It is humble, but it will be safe."

"Thank you."

She paused before leaving. "If I may ask, what brings you to the city on the eve of war?"

"Bad timing," I said. "And a search for someone." She nodded deeply and left it at that, excusing herself.

Getting settled took some doing. The odd noises and unfamiliar routine were hard to get past and now that I had a moment to think...

I pressed my palms into my eyes to stop the prickle of tears that threatened to fall. *Deep calming breaths. Stay focused.* But it didn't work.

A sob tore from my throat and I curled up into the fetal position on my cot, holding my blanket to my mouth to stifle my cries.

I was scared. I just wanted Gareth here, next to me. Even a hint of our bond would've comforted me, but it was radio silence. I just hoped he was truly okay, wherever he was.

The morning dawned with a clear blue sky, not a cloud in sight. By early afternoon, the heat was becoming oppressive.

I hadn't seen the priestess that morning when I set out, but an acolyte knew to keep an eye out for me and handed me a small token before I left.

"So when you return there won't be any issues if my mistress isn't here. Soldiers are returning and they gravitate here in times of trouble."

I couldn't tell exactly what he meant by that statement, if he was warning me that they'd try to keep me out or they'd try to keep me, period. With a small smile, I realized that I wasn't concerned either way. My abilities weren't limited to running away anymore. If a fight was instigated, I had full confidence I could handle myself.

So, with heatstroke a distinct possibility, I set out for another day of searching.

More people were streaming through the gates, the scent of fear growing heavier. Snatches of conversation revealed the Persians were moving fast. They'd chewed through several city-states, razing them and moving on to the next. Their military might was fixed on Athens for the second time in a decade, and the name Xerxes preceded it all.

Around midday, sweat pooling between my shoulder blades and my hair stuck tight to my scalp, I gravitated toward one of the community wells. Intent on waiting in the shade for a drink and taking a moment to rest, commotion preempted that thought. A man was expelled from a nearby hostel, a large bouncer-type pulling an equally tall but much slimmer man out the door by the collar of his robe.

The person being booted onto the street had his hands in the air and muttered something too low to hear over the crowds watching and gossiping. Despite the heat, he was covered head to toe in that robe, the hood pulled up and shielding his face from view. I glimpsed a long, sharp nose and sculpted cheekbone before the man tripped into the street.

The proprietor was hovering in the darkness of the doorway, hand on hips. "Never come here again, you disgrace." He sneered before disappearing into the hostel. The muscle followed and the door slammed shut.

This man was hunched, shoulders bowed as he scurried from the throngs of people still watching him. He tripped on a crate and went sprawling, his long arms and legs a tangle as he landed on the ground. The people surrounding him laughed and jeered, kicking at him.

Something about him called to me, but this couldn't be the person I was looking for. He didn't stand up to them or even give the crowd a dirty look. He picked himself up with a massive effort, and went on his way, taking a side alley and zipping out of sight.

I looked back at the welcoming shade and the potential for a drink of cold water, sighed, and followed.

The alley he'd taken was stuffed with people setting up shelters. It was near all the amenities they'd need, making it prime real estate as the city continued to fill.

Over the last day, at least two battalions of hoplites filed into the city along with everyone else. The barracks filled with raucous and nervous soldiers, waiting for the enemy that would soon be at the gates.

I kept enough distance that I wouldn't be spotted, always letting the man stay at least twenty paces ahead. I lost him a couple of times, but only for a moment.

I exited onto a promenade that skirted the training ground around the barracks. Most of the soldiers were patrolling and civilians weren't allowed any closer to their quarters, so this district was much quieter. Which also meant I could get a better, unadulterated sense of the man I was following.

There was a hint of something there. I sensed his signature, but there was a block of some kind dulling it. As I watched him slink away, clutching his hood tighter and shying away from anyone that got too near, I was even more drawn to follow.

I was in full spy mode, peeking around the corner just enough to see. Citizens were banned from this area, but I'd risk it to keep him in sight. Ahead of me, the man abruptly turned into an alley so narrow it was barely wide enough for two people to walk side by side and almost completely shaded.

He found his destination, darting through a slim doorway after a furtive glance around to make sure nobody was watching. I inched forward and peeked through a small window, shutters open just enough that I could see it was a store room with preserves, garlands of onions and garlic, and sacks of milled wheat.

The man was looking around on the shelves, picking through the food stuffs and secreting items he liked in his pockets. There was a rope of dried meat on a high hook and when he reached to grab it, his hood fell back. When I caught sight of him, I gasped, then immediately ducked down as the man turned toward me. I heard movement and shuffling, but it was at a steady pace, so I didn't think he'd seen me. A quick peek confirmed he was back to pilfering the shelves.

The room was small, and I only saw one entrance, so I decided to wait. There was a stack of amphora, taller than me and three times as wide, against the wall under a canopy. The thick clay was cool, and I nestled between them, sighing at the unexpected relief. I could keep watch on the door, and still be concealed.

When I picked up the chatter of voices, I pushed back farther into my hiding space. I cocked my head, curious, when I realized one of the voices was female. She sounded flirty, giggling and teasing as the man she was with grumbled something about the location.

They came into view, the woman wearing short robes and sandals and a hair covering that looked like large-gauge mesh, her dark black curls heavily oiled and spilling around a face bright with makeup. The man looked around and, seeming satisfied they were alone, moved her farther into the alley. He motioned for her to spin around, but she shook her head and held out her hand.

"Money first," she said.

"I'm not paying you up front," the soldier grumbled. "Turn around."

She simply stared and continued to hold out her hand, completely unbothered by his threatening manner.

"Fine," he said, taking coins from his pocket and placing them in her hand.

"This isn't what we agreed on."

"He folded his arms. "Take it or leave it, won't be hard to find another woman." The words were gruff and menacing, but I got the impression that they knew each other.

I could see my target's shape still moving in the storeroom, but a small sound made me turn. The woman's robes were bunched around her waist and the soldier's sword belt hit the ground.

My eyes widened and I spun away, crouching lower and facing the wall. I couldn't leave, or they'd see me.

It felt so intrusive to be listening to their tryst. I'd never been one for voyeurism and I could feel the heat of embarrassment in my cheeks. When the pair had quieted, I risked a glance, first across the alley to check on my target, and then to see if the coast was clear to move.

They were straightening themselves up and the woman turned her head, eyes catching mine. I froze, terrified she'd give me away, but she only gave me a wink and licked her upper lip with a quick swipe of her tongue.

My face flamed even hotter and she gave me a wicked smile before looking away.

The woman traced her finger along the soldier's jaw as they headed back the way they'd come. "You never disappoint."

He slapped her ass with a chuckle. "Don't forget that."

When they turned the corner, I left the shade and coolness of my hiding spot and ventured forward, peeking through the shutters of the storeroom.

"Shit." I pushed the door open and looked inside. There had been another door I couldn't see from the window, one hidden between the shelves. It opened into a courtyard in plain view of anyone in the barracks, so no way in hell was I going that way.

Twenty minutes later, I returned to the community well where I'd initially seen the man, cursing my luck. I'd scoured the restricted areas as best I could, but there was no trace of him. Now I was starting from scratch.

# CHAPTER EIGHT

# Meg

Dejected, I returned to the temple. Maybe the priestess would have some ideas. The shadows were growing long as I reached the Acropolis. Hoplites had started to make their way up, and I could feel their stares trailing after me as I neared the Propylaea.

A small group, all wearing full gear with helmets under their arms, stepped in front of me as I moved to mount the steps.

"The temple is closed. Our lady is only hearing soldier's prayers."

I stared him in the eye, unflinching. "Then it's a good thing I'm not here to pray or make offerings. I'm staying with the enclave."

Another soldier spoke, sounding like his voice only changed yesterday. "But you're a civilian."

"Not quite." I made to push past them, but they held their arms in a blockade.

"I don't care what you are. Leave," said the first. "This is now a place to prepare for death."

Knowing what was about to happen, how this city would be razed and this temple destroyed by Xerxes's army, I didn't respond. I pulled the token out of the pouch at my side and showed it to him, making sure the light from the fires gave him a good look.

He snatched my wrist and pulled my hand closer, studying the small signet with narrowed eyes. "Who'd you steal this from?"

I sighed. "An acolyte handed this to me personally, as a token to get past you if you gave me a hard time."

He sneered and his buddies crowded in around him. "Is that so?"

This was going to get ugly if this douche didn't unhand me.

"What's the trouble here?" asked a soft voice.

We all turned toward the source, the same priestess I'd met the night before coming up the path behind me. She cocked her head and the soldier, still not releasing my wrist, became nervous. "She stole this signet and tried to claim that it was you that gave it to her."

Without any shift in her demeanor at all, the priestess said, "I did give it to her. I'd assumed it would keep her safe. Clearly I was wrong." A chill ran down my spine, maybe even a prickle of fear at her cold tone.

The soldier released me like he'd been burned. To the priestess, he stammered, "My apologies, Philomena."

The priestess's eyes flicked to me and back to the soldier. "I'm not the one who requires an apology."

"My apologies, miss. Won't happen again."

I stared at him coldly and brushed past him, climbing the stairs with the priestess falling into step beside me. Once we were safely inside the gates, I asked, "Why do they seem afraid of you?"

The ghost of a smile slid across her face before disappearing. "Another lifetime." She glanced in the direction of the temple. "Before Lady Athena called me to serve her."

I couldn't not tell her what was coming for the city. "Do you know what Xerxes is capable of?" I asked quietly.

She nodded. "Far too well."

"If I told you that I'm certain this city will be destroyed, would you leave?"

She shook her head and smiled sadly. "This is my place, no matter the end." When the silence had stretched just longer than was comfortable, she jerked her head to the side. "Come. Join me for a meal. I'd like to learn more about you."

The other members of the temple were in far different spirits than the citizens and soldiers in the city. Calm reigned supreme. Demure smiles, knowing glances, softly spoken words. Not a single panicked outcry or worried glance.

When we reached a banquet area, several other members of Athena's cult sat around the small chamber, conversing quietly among themselves. Either their faith was strong, or they weren't afraid to die in the service of their lady.

The meal was a simple one of highly spiced, roasted meat and a flatbread made with lard that had my mouth watering. The wine was strong but—smoke 'em if you got 'em. No sense in holding anything back.

"You said you were looking for someone?" asked Philomena.

"Yes. The only name I have is Andrus."

"Not exactly a rare name," she admitted, sipping her wine.

"No," I admitted. "It certainly isn't." I thought of the best way I could describe him, but I only had the brief glimpse I'd caught to go off of. I gave Philomena a rundown of what I remembered, but she only frowned.

There would certainly be traits they'd all have in common, so I tried that instead. "He's a man of high bearing, if not high stature. Carries himself with honor but also humility. Cares for the people around him. Probably not an egotistical asshole, but has his moments."

"Any idea what kind of position he may hold? Profession?"

"A leader. Someone that people trust and aspire to be. He'll make them feel safe." My heart twisted as Rowan's face flashed through my mind. They should've been safe. Gareth would've fought the whole human army if he hadn't been more concerned about getting me to safety. "He fought alongside the Titans in another life. One of their most trusted allies."

Philomena nodded. "Now that rings a bell."

I stopped chewing and stared at the priestess intently.

"I knew an Andrus Telemachus when I still moved among the elite factions of this city. He fits every description you just gave me. About a year back, word began spreading about a disgrace he'd suffered. He was a great man, everyone thought he would be aligned to become a general with any outfit he desired. But he disappeared. There were only rumors after that, he'd gone mad, ran off with the archon's daughter, threw himself into the sea. All the favorites."

"What kind of disgrace?"

Philomena shrugged. "Any truth was lost to the stories, same as his fate. I have a very hard time believing any of it. Andrus was one of the most honorable men I knew at court. I can't imagine anything short of slighting one of the gods would have gotten him in trouble." She raised a delicately sculpted brow, a thought occurring to her. "Although, given his affiliations, that seems like a very reasonable possibility."

"Any idea where someone with his kind of background might be lurking? If he were trying to stay away from curious folks?"

Philomena snorted, a sound that seemed out of place coming from her. "I'd start with the taverns. I can direct you to an old acquaintance of mine. She's probably the best source of information outside of court spies."

I raised my wine in a salute before taking a sip. "That would be much appreciated."

I waited until the sun was well on its way toward the horizon before setting out the next evening. My day was spent getting steadily more frustrated with my inability to track down Gareth or approach even a semblance of a trance state. I was cursing up such a blue streak, some of the acolytes thought I might've been possessed by a crazed god with a message and went to fetch one of the priestesses to interpret.

Once they'd left my chamber, shaking their heads and disappointed, the silence was heavy with emptiness. I'd always had a home base to return to before Bel's true nature was revealed. And then after I'd met Gareth... I had a home in him. I escaped to him, I found calm and security in him. I don't think I would've realized that I was caught in Hypnos's illusions so quickly, if at all, if I hadn't been so certain that Gareth would *never* hurt me.

I'd never felt more alone than I did right now. Chasing ghosts. I couldn't lose him. I *would not* lose him.

A warm drop of liquid on my bare foot surprised me out of my thoughts and I realized I was crying. I swiped at my tears, frustrated, pushing to my feet. Find Andrus, then get Gareth back.

Keep going.

The soldiers that had tried to stop me the night before were nowhere to be seen as I descended the Propylaea steps, and others gave me a wide berth. The crowds that filled the city streets soon swallowed me up, and I went with the flow of traffic until I reached the quarter that Philomena pointed to as the usual haunt for the neighborhood gossip.

But it wasn't long before I regretted my choice to leave so late in the day. The shadows fell thick and fast, and my wolf hovered closer to the surface, ready for imminent danger. I tried to soothe my nerves as best I could, but in a city before streetlights, where the only illumination came from braziers outside of taverns and brothels, the dark corners and alleys became much more sinister. The moon wasn't even that bright tonight, so my night vision didn't have much to work with.

The woman I was looking for would be near one of the brothels. There were several owned by the same madame, so this woman could be at any of them. Philomena said I would know her by the distinctive acropolis flower she always wore in her hair wrap.

A soft groan made me whirl around toward the alley I'd just passed. In the dim shadows I could just make out shapes, my eyes adjusting quickly to the edge of darkness. One of the figures looked in my direction and I stammered a quick "Sorry," before scuttling away, tripping on the iron leg of a brazier and almost sprawling face-first to the ground.

A light laugh made me turn. "You aren't from around here, are you?"

The woman that spoke leaned against the wall outside a brothel. She wore shorter skirts and her lips were painted a vivid red, hair coiffed and bundled into a finely woven mesh netting, a green, leafy stem with tiny purple flowers resting next to her ear. I stared, dumbfounded. Had I really found my quarry already?

She smiled. "Now I know you aren't from here. You're making too much eye contact."

I blinked. "Sorry," I said again. I nodded my head back in the direction of the alley. "Caught me by surprise."

"No need to be embarrassed." The woman pushed away from the wall and sauntered toward me. "It's fun to watch."

A sparkle in her eye made me realize with a punch to the gut that this was the woman I'd seen with the soldier. Heat flooded my face as I tried to stammer out an explanation. She laughed, good natured and waved her hand. "The city is pretty crowded these days, hard to find privacy." Her eyes narrowed. "Although, I wonder what you were doing that close to a restricted area? Since you clearly weren't there in a professional capacity." She frowned at me. "A real waste."

My eyes widened, mortified. "I—I was looking for someone."

"Are you planning on wandering the city all night to find them?" The woman raised her eyebrows, perfectly outlined and plucked. Her seductive smile turned to passing disinterest at the change of topic.

"I have it on good authority that you're the woman that can help me find him. Philomena sent me."

Her eyebrow peaked even higher. "Did she?" She scoffed and went to turn away, but I pulled out the signet I was still carrying and showed it to her. She snatched my wrist much like the soldier had and studied it closely. It seemed to satisfy her because she settled back against the wall. "What's the name of this person you're after?"

"Andrus."

When she realized I wasn't going to offer more information, she frowned. "Is there a last name?"

"Possibly Telemachus?"

I gave her the same description I'd given Philomena, along with the priestess's suspicions of who Andrus was.

The woman looked thoughtful. "You might be in luck. I heard he's been haunting the west end. He's been using the taverns as his only port of call these days."

My heart leaped; this sounded promising.

Sensing my excitement, she quickly squashed it. "But you can't go there tonight. It's far too dangerous. That's the worst part of the city. Only a fool would go there at night and only a woman with a death wish would go there alone."

I nodded, not that I had any intention of heeding her warning. There were plenty of Strangers in this city that would be a match for me with my new abilities, but I couldn't stop searching being this close. I'd always been hard-wired with a sense of urgency, even when there was a good chance it would only cause trouble.

"Thank you."

A group of men came out of the tavern and she pushed away from the wall. She glided over to them and wrapped her arm around one, then another, as they gave her hungry stares. There was a brief negotiation, and she led one of them toward a small side door into a mudbrick building. With a last look back at me, she smiled. "Tell Philomena that I'll be looking to her for a favor."

# CHAPTER NINE

## *Meg*

The west end of the city was indeed the most raucous, and I cursed. A brawl spilled out of a tavern on my right, and I flinched back, barely avoiding getting swept into the melee. I dashed to the side of the street and skirted the crowds, moving into the flow of people. The taverns were filled to capacity, the patrons hoping to drink away their impending doom.

There were so many, and after a particularly hairy run-in with a group of men too drunk to heed their sense of self-preservation, I settled for popping my head through the windows or peeking around doors and scanning the rooms. Anything promising would elicit a closer look, but I had too much ground to cover to take it slow.

I already suspected who I was looking for and given the heat even during this time of night, if he was still wearing his cloak to conceal himself, he would be easy to spot.

The third tavern on this stretch of road was also one of the nicer ones—although the standards meant it had the least amount of vomit and human waste around it.

A quick scan of the interior and I was about ready to head back out into the night, but a flicker of recognition made me do a double take. Was that his signature I'd felt just now?

A small table squatted in a corner of the room, the man hunched over his drink hiding within the hood of his cloak. That was him. I couldn't see much other than a flash of bronze skin and dark blond hair curled around his face.

Cautiously, I moved toward him. His eyes were half-closed in a drunken stupor. I'd made the mistake of passing too close to a table, and a man attempted to scoop me up and set me on his lap. My yelp of surprise drew more than a few stares, including one from Andrus. Our eyes locked for just a moment and I could see recognition in his face, before the man's hand started groping under my clothes.

After a precariously poised claw threatened his manhood, the drunk let me go with a muttered apology. I stood and straightened myself up, hoping my first impression wasn't ruined. But he was gone.

I hurried over to the table where he'd been sitting, looking for another exit. A breeze gusted through the room, and I followed it to an open window, the shutters flung outward. It looked out onto a smaller side street, still at ground level, so I hopped out and took my best guess where he would've gone.

The street was crowded, a few food vendors having set up stalls and drawing half-stumbling patrons like zombies to the smell of roasting meat.

I caught sight of Andrus pushing through a group of people and I hurried after him, for once glad that my small stature allowed me to move more easily in the crush of bodies. I'd just slipped between a swarm of converging friends laughing and greeting one another and stopped. Behind me, raucous crowds of people. In front of me, nothing but a muted, dark street.

Shit.

My wolf moved forward, scouting for danger as I took tentative steps. The dark swallowed me up as I stepped away from the last remnants of cheery firelight burning behind me. A heavy step, followed by another, and another, and a figure moved into a shaft of light breaking into the narrow street.

I was met with a scarred face and gleaming, jagged teeth.

"You," I snarled, backpedaling. Two more forms appeared from the darkness that were far less human than the first. My wolf frantically tried to make sense of the situation. Everything about the first man screamed mortal, even if he was terrifying. But the other two forms were demons, and yet they weren't. They were just shadows of demons, at half their power, if that.

"Do you like my pets?" The man motioned at the demons. "Members of my menagerie. Just like you will be."

Then I understood what I was looking at. "A human sorcerer?"

The man nodded, his broken grin widening. He'd summoned the demons and ripped their souls from their bodies. These creatures were just shades the process had left behind. Powerful and fast, with no ability to refuse an order, They were the perfect henchmen.

They were also all but impossible to destroy unless I killed their master first, and since I'd have to go through those two to do it, I was putting my chances of success at *limited*.

My claws extended, and I allowed my jaw to transform into the perfect weapon for ripping out throats. I'd have to settle for disabling the shades as best I could, tearing them to pieces and hoping it slowed them down. Even in my wolf form, I wouldn't be able to outrun them.

The sorcerer laughed. "A nice trick. People will pay a lot of money to see you."

I growled and lunged forward, tackling the first shade and punching my claws into its chest, tearing a hole through it before biting into its shoulder. I wrenched at the joint, about to rip its arm off, when the other shade flew at me and grabbed me around the waist, hauling me away. It held me tight to its chest and my feet kicked uselessly off the ground. I couldn't get any traction to attack. My claws dug into anything I could reach, but it didn't feel pain. It didn't even flinch.

I howled in frustration and struggled as hard as I could, reaching, grabbing, kicking. The shade easily walked me to its master, who awaited me with hand outstretched, power crackling between his fingers as he prepared a spell to knock me out.

A sword swung out of nowhere, cutting the sorcerer's arm off at the elbow. He barely had time to scream before the sword took his head off and the body slumped to the ground, blood splashing across the stone.

The shades faltered. Quicker than my eyes could follow, the wraiths were cut to pieces, dissolving into nothing. The shade holding me dropped me to the ground, and I landed on hands and feet, lunging at its knees to take it down. A hand grabbed my arm and yanked me back, my rescuer stepping in front of me and repeating the same actions on the remaining shade.

Everything fell silent. Now that I wasn't in battle mode, it was obvious that Andrus had come to my rescue, even if I couldn't see the same golden curls or sharp features. He was panting and I could see his hand shaking, sword quivering, before he tossed it aside.

He rounded on me so suddenly, I lurched back a step. His face held an expression of pure devastation as he stared at me.

My gaze roved over him. The slump of his shoulders, the way he averted his eyes, the hands that didn't know what to do with themselves as they clenched and unclenched at his sides.

I raised my hand and reached forward. Andrus froze, but didn't pull away or try to stop me, and I placed my hand in the center of his chest.

Seeking for the connection that bound us together, I found it tangled with someone else's magick. It wasn't Titanic in origin. It was an Ætherim.

"Andrus," I said, waiting for him to look at me.

Shakily, he turned his head and met my eyes for a brief second, long enough for me to know he was listening.

"Whose magick is on you?"

His whole body flinched, and he sidestepped to get away. Andrus walked off down the alley, heading for the crowds again.

"Wait!" He kept going, and thanks to his much longer gait, I had a hard time keeping up with him. "Andrus, stop!" He darted around a corner and lost himself in the crowd. I jumped up on the nearest vendor stand, eliciting startled yells as I scrambled up a low wall to look over the mass of people from a higher vantage point. He was gone.

Someone else's magick held him under its influence. How could I break it? I'd never dealt with curses or any kind of binding magick, especially when it seemed to have been put in place by a very capable god.

Dawn was on the horizon. People had gathered around the Acropolis, staring over the city walls as I trudged back to the temple in defeat. Immersed in my own self-pity, it took me a moment to recognize the murmurs and soft crying punctuating the stillness as families clung together. I stopped and joined them at the walls.

My stomach clenched as I got a glimpse of what was causing their fear.

Xerxes's armies had arrived.

"That's just the vanguard," said Philomena. "The rest of his forces are at least two days away."

Activity buzzed throughout the temple as the priestesses and acolytes assisted visitors and held vigil, a constant stream of prayers and offerings as they plead to Athena for mercy and victory.

The "vanguard" was massive, and they surrounded the city in a slow, unbothered maneuver practiced many times before. I'd stuck close to the temple for the last couple of days, planning my next moves. I needed to be ready when I ran into Andrus for any problems that might arise. It might be the last chance I'd get to break whatever spell was over him before the Persians started their assault on the city. I couldn't see how an army this massive would be content to hold a long siege.

During the night and early dawn, screams punctuated the uneasy quiet that settled over Athens, people still traveling to the city for safety arriving too late, caught by the invaders. Smoke rose in the distance, the marching armies burning as they went, leaving a trail for the rest to follow and starting a terror campaign that was gripping the city.

Once the rest of his troops arrived, it would be the end. Nobody was getting out.

"Aren't there tunnels?" I asked Philomena. "Some kind of escape route?"

She shook her head, grim. "They were sealed up after the last siege, two decades ago. The enemy found the passages and used them against us."

"These people are going to die," I said, barely able to comprehend the scale of the destruction that was coming. "And the ones that don't will wish they had."

"May Athena wreath us in glory, even if it's in the afterlife."

I bit my tongue and resisted the urge to argue with her. "What can you tell me about binding magick? Any idea how to break a curse placed by a god?"

Philomena blinked a few times. "Does this have anything to do with Andrus?"

I nodded.

"You believe the gods cursed him?"

Another nod. After a moment of thought, she led the way to a small library filled with scrolls. Toward the back corner was a section so old and brittle, I was afraid to handle anything.

"These are some of the oldest records here. Most are trivial, but if I remember correctly there are some that talk about the old rituals and magicks performed here, along with quite a few records of the various curse tablets left around the Acropolis over the generations."

A shriek warbled through the air, overwhelmed fear splintering off from a prayer. It wasn't the first we'd heard that day, or that hour.

"If you'll excuse me," said Philomena. She hurried off, and I was left alone with the dusty scrolls.

I had to come up for air once the dust had crusted in my nostrils and the spiders weren't content to just watch from the sidelines as I worked. All I'd found so far that might prove useful were old methods of intercession magick. Breaking someone else's curse by overloading it with something stronger.

The fresh air I'd been expecting as I reached the top of the stairs was tainted with smoke. My brow furrowed and as I walked into the late evening courtyard, chaos met me.

"What's happened?" I asked a passing acolyte.

"The rest of the army arrived. They're already moving to breach the walls."

Before I could ask any follow-up questions, the acolyte gave me an apologetic look and hurried on.

Most of the guard that had taken up residence on the Acropolis had moved out, but several still lined the roads leading up to the Propylaea, maintaining order as people surged to make their pleas to Athena.

"Meg!" shouted Philomena. I raced to the wall where the priestess was gazing down the curving path of the Acropolis to the crossroads where it met with the city streets. As soon as I was near, she flung her arm out and pointed at a commotion, a small group of armed guards attempting to keep Andrus at bay as he fought to get past them.

It was strange to watch and I could tell Philomena didn't know what to make of it, either. Andrus would attack and clumsily scrabble to get past the guard before backing away, almost like another force was pulling him off. He would lose focus and wander for a moment before seeming to remember what he was there for and launching into another attack.

"The curse is fighting him," she said, her eyes narrowed. There was something in her gaze that made me think she was seeing something that I couldn't. "He's trying to get to you and it's forcing him back."

"I have to go," I said to her. A shriek sounded from the outer defense wall of the city and a loud crash followed. The ground beneath my feet shook and Xerxes's army roared. Philomena hid her fear well, but I could smell it oozing off her. "Are you sure I can't convince you to get out?"

She shook her head and remained silent.

"Please be careful."

Philomena gave a sideways smile and revealed a small dagger hidden in her robes. "I'll be fine."

"That won't do much good against an army," I murmured.

"It only has to take one life." Her fingers caressed the hilt before she hid it away. "Go. Good luck."

My throat constricted as I nodded. She grabbed my hand, and I squeezed it back, her fingers slipping away as I vaulted the stone retaining wall and dropped fifteen feet to the road below. I ran down the winding path until I reached the guard, reengaged with Andrus as he fought tooth and nail—

I stopped in my tracks as two fangs extended from his upper incisors, dripping with saliva. Andrus lunged and grabbed the nearest guard, wrenching his head to the side while his mouth opened in a wide snarl.

"Andrus!" I shouted. He froze an inch from the guard's neck. Nothing moved except for his eyes as they roamed to my face, a bright, blood-red ring surrounding his irises. "Let him go," I said.

The guards had all backed away at my approach and the man in Andrus's clutches plead with me silently for help. I stepped to Andrus and placed a hand lightly on his shoulder. His reaction was immediate, but instead of lunging at me, he dropped his hold on the guard and flung himself away, hurrying toward the crowds to get away from me.

People no longer moved freely through the city, choosing instead to huddle next to walls and under cover, many with eyes closed as they spoke silent prayers.

That made it much easier to keep Andrus in my sights as I chased him down. I could easily outpace Gareth; I made up for in speed what he had in size. But Andrus was fast and his stride was much longer than mine so I was sprinting to keep up.

People were shrinking away as we barreled past. "Stop!" I shouted.

He faltered but kept running, and I put a little more sauce on the words, a command. "Stop!"

He jerked to a halt, and I caught him. I wrapped my hands in his cloak and jerked him toward me, staring him in the eye.

"Can you at least tell me which god might have done this? I don't need to know the why." I just wanted to know how hard it was going to be to get past the curse's defenses.

Andrus shook his head. "Can't." He reached out, hesitant, and cupped my face with a trembling hand. The tenderness and longing in his touch were plain, emotions warring on his face. His eyes would darken with blank confusion before clearing up and staring at me with wonder. But the minute he fell too far into those feelings, the binding of the curse took over and had him struggling to get out of my grip again.

We must've made quite a sight. The top of my head only came up to his chest and his build screamed *fighter*, but my waif of a self was holding him in place, glaring daggers as I planned my strike.

Our connection was supposed to be stronger than anything. The Titans forged it. The Desma were bound to the Titans first, and I was created with that same magick. It should override anything else that tried to interfere. Theoretically.

The curse was clouding his mind, no question, and semi-controlling his actions. But it didn't go deep enough to make him forget about me or his purpose.

So maybe I needed to give him a reminder, loud and clear, about what was important.

Andrus was no longer struggling and stared into space. I didn't release my grip on him and called my power forward. The last time I'd tried to focus it like this, Gareth had disappeared into time. My hands shook. Doubt took over as I imagined Andrus vanishing out of existence. Was there another way? My breathing quickened in panic.

I needed more time to figure this out, I couldn't afford to mess this up again.

*Trust yourself.* That's what Kronos had said.

With a deep breath, I directed my magick into my palm, feeling the weight of it as it sizzled, crackling, waiting to be set loose.

His curse sensed a change and his eyes snapped toward me. Before he could act, I thrust my hand dead center over his heart, unleashing every bit of essence that I could spare into him.

Pure shock crossed his face, and he stilled. Warmth spread from my hand and I felt his heartbeat racing under my palm, sweat forming on his skin. A jolt of electricity flowed between us and wind whipped up out of nowhere, blowing away the last remnants of the curse's residue before falling still again.

I was shaking, and we were both breathing heavily. Andrus wrapped his hand around mine and lowered it from his chest, thumb tracing my palm. He was staring at me and the city around him with a bemused expression. Actually *seeing* things for the first time in I didn't know how long.

"Are you okay?" I asked.

He refocused on me and heaved a breath. Andrus made a choked sound deep in his throat and I stepped back in alarm when he dropped to his knees, still gripping my hand. He crept forward and wrapped his arms around my waist and I instinctively laid my hand on his head. Face buried in my stomach, his whole body shook as a sob tore from his throat.

"You freed me." Andrus gripped me tighter, and we stayed like that until he calmed. At last, he pulled away and looked at me, reaching up and running a gentle thumb across my cheek. "It's really you."

He stood and straightened, rolling his shoulders back as his whole bearing changed, transforming into a new man before my eyes. He was taller than Gareth, but built less like a warrior and more like a martial arts practitioner, all deadly grace and speed. His angular features softened as he smiled, and his natural confidence returned.

This was more in line with what I would have expected from the man I was searching for.

I had butterflies in my stomach all over again as I offered him a tentative smile. "I'm sorry it took me so long."

Andrus leaned in and placed a light kiss on my lips. "You're here now."

I stood on my tiptoes and leaned in for another kiss as a horn blasted in the distance.

# CHAPTER TEN

# Andrus

S he'd done it. My dark angel, arriving at my lowest and pulling me from the grip of the curse. I'd given up hope that I'd ever reunite with my brothers and be able to join in the fight for victory. Ever since Mithras had cursed me, I'd been wandering in a daze, unable to form coherent thoughts. I was missing large amounts of time from my memory. Sometimes I could only tell how long it had been since I was last conscious of my actions by the growth of the stubble on my face.

And I'd have to wonder what I'd done that resulted in the blood crusted under my fingernails or the newly formed scars on my body.

In those lucid moments, all I could do was grieve the loss of my family and friends and avoid the mocking stares of my countrymen and former allies as they whispered about my failures and fall from grace. The only thing that kept me going was my dedication to the Titans, the ever-present drive that kept me from falling completely under the thumb of the curse.

When she, Megiste, had walked into that tavern, my mind cleared for the first time in years. She was everything the Titans had promised and more. Megiste was touched by the Fates, her soul glowed with it, calling to me. Our future together spread out before me in a rapid-fire kaleidoscope of images of what *could* happen if I took her hand and stood by her side.

Through the darkness, I heard her name in my head, and when I'd met her eyes... I couldn't stand the thought of her seeing me like that.

So I ran.

But she chased me and didn't give up. When the armies arrived at the city walls, the curse had taken hold of me again. Without her presence to keep me focused, I lost myself, but her magick called to me, leading me to her even if I wasn't conscious of it.

The beginning of the attack on the city spurred me into action, and I'd had to fight against myself and anyone that got in my way as I tried to find her.

My fingers clasped behind her head as I stared into her eyes. Had she said something?

I blinked. "I'm sorry?"

She huffed out a small laugh, and her hand rested on my wrist as she smiled. "Who cursed you?"

I faltered and dropped my hand. "It's a long story." She looked at me with an annoyed quirk of her lips. "One that I will take all the time needed to tell in full, I promise."

The reality of our situation had been sinking in. We were surrounded by Xerxes's army, and we had to escape a city under siege.

A loud crash sounded from the direction of the west gates and screams echoed up from the refugees huddled in the streets, spreading through them like a wave as the fear became contagious. People surged to their feet and ran or hid as the clash of weapons rang out.

How had they breeched the gates so fast?

"Hold on," said Megiste. Magick kindled and sputtered out and she swore. "I found you, why can't we leave?"

I took Megiste's hand and pulled her after me through the streets, toward the east side of the city.

"Where are we going?" she shouted.

"We have to find a way out." If my memory was correct, there was one way we could still get past the army.

We were about halfway toward our goal when the crowds grew thicker and we had to push our way through, almost getting separated.

"Can we go up?" asked Megiste. "Run on the roofs?"

"Maybe, but some of those jumps are long."

She smiled. "Don't worry about that."

I wasn't sure what her plan was, but she seemed confident. "Up it is, then."

We backtracked to where I'd seen massive amphorae outside a warehouse. I lifted Megiste onto the tallest one and she jumped to catch the lip of the roof, swinging herself up. After I'd joined her, I pointed out the path we needed to take

She considered it and removed her clothing, balling it up and handing it to me. I didn't have time to ask what she was doing before she transformed into a breathtaking wolf. I could only stare in amazement before she barked at me and took off, me following close behind.

In that form, she leaped across distances between buildings without even the slightest hesitation, clearing them easily. I had a hard time keeping up and almost missed a couple of the longer jumps.

By the time we ran out of rooftops, we were near our destination.

"The palace?" she asked.

I nodded. The crowds weren't as thick here, the palace guard making things far from hospitable for the people who wanted to set up camp nearby, but it was quickly filling as chaos set in and people had nowhere else to go.

Megiste shifted back to her human form, and I handed her her clothes, attempting not to stare. She wasn't bothered either way.

I jumped off the roof and held out my arms as she dangled on the edge before dropping. Her floral scent enveloped me, and I didn't want to let her go.

"Andrus," she said, humor in her gaze.

I reluctantly set her down and grabbed her hand, leading her to a small passage that ran alongside the palace wall before reaching a gated entrance that servants used. It was always guarded and barricaded, but now it was just the barricade that we'd need to get through.

I made quick work of the locks and was battering my way through the door itself when a fireball erupted in the distance.

"Was that from the good guys or the bad guys?" she asked, crowding a little closer to me. A new cacophony of screams rose in answer. "Oh," she breathed.

The door shattered inward into a dark tunnel, and I pulled her with me, slamming the door shut behind us.

"Where are we going?"

"There should still be an escape tunnel near here."

"Philomena said they'd all been blocked up."

I shook my head. "The elite wouldn't leave themselves with no means of escape."

We followed the passage in the dark, my hand skimming the wall in front of me, until it opened out into the lowest level of the palace. It smelled musty and wet, puddles of water forming in the pocked stone floor. The space was eerily quiet. Maybe they'd already fled. We moved cautiously into the chamber, just a few low fires to give off any light.

"Are you here to hurt us?" a small voice asked.

I heard Meg gasp and turned to see several families huddled against the wall. A little boy had spoken and his mother snatched him back up in her arms, her eyes wide and terrified.

"No," said Megiste, softly. "We're looking for a way out."

My heart sank. If they were still here, then maybe the passage was gone.

"There is no way out," a man spat. "The tunnel's collapsed. We're trapped."

"Where is it?" asked Megiste.

"Over there, but it won't do you any good," a woman said, pointing.

Megiste hurried to the tunnel, and I followed close behind.

"Shit," I hissed. The tunnel mouth was visible just beyond a tumble of rock and debris.

It didn't seem to faze Megiste. She ran her hands along the rocks and closed her eyes, focusing on something. Her mouth pulled into a frown and she opened her eyes again.

"What are you thinking?" I asked.

"I'm wondering if I can make something work."

I looked at her quizzically.

"I tried transporting us through time but I'm still blocked off. But the kind of magick I'm going to use now works a bit different. It's all localized. I've only done it once before, though." Her gaze shot to me and back to the rocks. "I kind of disappeared someone—"

"What?"

"—but since I'm not using this technique on a person this time, I don't think I'll be quite so stressed."

I didn't know what to say, so I just watched her. I could feel the others in the chamber with us creep closer as they grew curious. None of my instincts were telling me they were a threat, so I kept my focus on Megiste.

The first inklings of magick sparked. It felt heavy, like a gusty wind in a small space. The debris started to rumble and footsteps behind me scurried away as the whole chamber shook.

Before my eyes, the rocks shifted, moving backward and seating themselves back in the walls of the tunnel. By the time her magick ebbed away, the tunnel was clear.

The trapped servants erupted in gasps and sobs of relief as they moved forward, cautiously glancing at Megiste. They were glad of an escape route, but terrified of her. Anger simmered through me as I wrapped an arm around her. She was shaking from her efforts.

"Go," I said, jerking my head at the tunnel.

Without a word of thanks, they ran. When I heard the last of their footfalls disappear, I crouched in front of Megiste. "That was incredible. How did you do that?"

She gave me a tired smile. "A new trick I just learned. We should move. I'm not sure if it'll hold."

I nodded, and we were off once again, me in the lead just in case there were other surprises waiting for us ahead. When we came out the other end of the miles-long tunnel, we were on the beach, and the harbor was in sight. The group that had gone before us had taken their chances on land. Their footprints ran off in the opposite direction.

Night was falling and all I could focus on was getting to the harbor and finding a small craft to get us out of here. We could stick to the shoreline and find a safe harbor well away from Athens.

Screams from far too close startled me. Megiste jumped and whirled around.

"Fuck," she spat.

Behind us, a large troop of soldiers were marching into view, splintered off from the horde, and heading down the beach from the direction the servants had gone.

"We should run." At my suggestion, Megiste stripped down and transformed, sprinting forward with me right behind her.

Thunder cracked in the distance and I looked toward the clouds, the dark, billowing edge of a squall-line moving inland. We crested a rocky hill speckled with beach grass and slippery with sand. Immense waves broke against the sea walls of the harbor, making my escape plan far less appealing.

Regardless, I took the lead and headed right for the mooring docks. The roars of our pursuers carried ahead of them as they neared, a terrifying preview of what would come if they caught us. There were far too many to fight and we would have no way of funneling them or controlling their momentum if they attacked here.

I darted to a small boardwalk that led to the main runway, jutting out into the harbor and lined with small ships that ran shallow enough to anchor here. I chose a ship bobbing halfway down the line, looking small and uncertain in the growing squall, but it was the only one that was manageable with a crew of two people.

I motioned for Megiste to jump on just as the first raindrops fell. She transformed back, still standing on the dock, and grabbed her clothes, wrenching them over her head. "Are you kidding?" she asked. "We can't go out *there* in *this*." She motioned back and forth between the angry sea and ship. "It'll capsize the minute we hit open water."

"We don't have a whole lot of choice," I said. "But I'm very good at sailing." I forced a smile. "We'll be fine."

I hoped I'd kept the fear out of my voice. The army was getting close, and I again motioned for her to jump on as I piled the last of the rope onto the deck. The hull was shallow, the ship built for going on small runs, nothing that would require lodging or a massive amount of supplies. We wouldn't have much shelter against the elements, but we shouldn't have to be on the vessel for long.

She hesitated.

I held out my hand and looked at her, imploring.

"Please, Megiste. Trust me. I'll keep you safe."

She still looked dubious as she took another look at the ten-foot swells crashing toward shore. Ignoring my hand, she leaped into the bow, and I pushed us away from the dock as the first of the soldiers reached the gangway. We'd made it about thirty feet out into the water, but several jumped in after us.

"Why are they still pursuing us?" I asked, grabbing an oar to beat at one man as he neared the side.

"Bel must be influencing them somehow," she said. Another reached the side of the ship, a man with blank eyes and a twisted sneer. He attempted to claw his way up the side, fingernails gouging into the small creases between planks.

Megiste smashed the man in the face, sending him sprawling back into the water, arms spread wide and blood streaming from his nose. He went under, but surfaced, spluttering a moment later, blood running down his chin and dripping into the water. He howled in rage but turned back, the other few stronger swimmers deterred by this and turning back with him.

As we neared open water, I pulled the sails, lest the wind tear them to shreds and we ended up floating at the mercy of the current. I grabbed the rudder and held tight, praying it would keep us from getting swept away.

# CHAPTER ELEVEN

# Andrus

A nasty wave crashed over the bow and the boat dipped, taking on water faster than it was draining. I'd doomed us.

"What should I do?" Megiste yelled over the storm.

"Bail as much water as you can!" I shouted back, pointing at a bucket tied to the railing. I ripped the sword off my waist and strapped it down to the ship. I didn't want to risk losing it overboard, not if there was even a small chance that we'd make it out of this.

She scrambled over to it on her hands and knees, holding onto anything she could grab in between.

She scooped and poured, fighting what felt like a losing battle from the start as I strained to keep us straight in the water. This was it. It wouldn't be Bel or the other Ætherim to take us down in a blaze of glory. The sea would be the death of us.

I stared at Megiste, sick with anger at myself and fear for her as she continued to bail water, squinting her eyes against the pouring rain. Her hair was plastered to her face and whipping against her with stinging lashes as the wind took it.

I don't know what I was hoping for when I did it, but I made an entreaty to Oceanus, the words not audible over the gale, wind ripping them from my mouth as soon as they left it.

"Please. We're going to die out here. I know I failed her, but give us another chance. Please."

My hands shook, numb from nerves and the constant wash of cold water. I tasted blood and realized I'd bitten my lip so hard, I'd broken the skin. The boat visibly canted now.

I'd led her to her death. My job, first and foremost, was to keep her safe, and I failed spectacularly.

I screamed her name over the storm and she jerked her head toward me. I motioned to her, unwilling to release my hold on the rudder, but if this was it, I wanted her in my arms at the end. With a forlorn look at the hopeless task, she abandoned the bucket and sloshed through ankle deep water to my side. I swept her up in a one-armed embrace and put my lips against her ear.

"I'm sorry."

I crushed her to me, and she wrapped her arms around my neck, plastering herself to my side.

She shook her head. "This sucks." She choked out a laugh through her fear as the water rose higher and the ship tilted farther.

My shaky hand found her cheek and rested there, her skin cold. "Thank you for setting me free."

Another fork of lightning blasted across the sky, curling underneath the clouds and illuminating the sea of gigantic swells. Three massive waves bore down on us and I pulled Megiste's face into my chest so she wouldn't see them coming.

I closed my eyes and braced myself for the crash of water that would take us to the bottom of the sea. My shoulders hunched as I curled around her protectively, determined to at least shield her from the initial crash. But it never came.

I ventured a glance upward. The pelting rain was lightening, and the thunder had moved off in the distance. The water was placid as we drifted, the dark of night settling around us in the quiet ocean.

My voice was a whisper. "He heard me. He saved us."

Megiste stirred. "Who did?"

She stared around her, not believing the calm seas, let alone that we were alive.

"Oceanus. I called out to him for help."

She hummed. "Kronos said they have some of their magick available to them still. Now we just have to solve this problem," said Meg, freeing herself from my embrace and sloshing back over to the bucket, now floating in the deep water that was still dragging down our boat.

The little ship still canted severely. The odds that we'd get it to right weren't good. Even if it didn't capsize entirely, we'd be dead in the water.

"I don't suppose we're near a shipping lane?" asked Meg hopefully, already thinking of our potential need for rescue.

I looked around and my heart sank. "We won't find many ships sailing through these waters."

Megiste caught my tone of voice. "The way you said that makes me think it's not just being stranded that we need to worry about."

I shook my head. "No. Monsters plague these waters. This is central of their territory."

As if on cue, something heavy raked against the bottom of the ship, sending us both tumbling. The vibration of a subsonic call rose from the water, setting my teeth on edge. The boat shivered and Meg scrambled away from the edge of the deck as a huge, dark shape appeared.

Its body was massive, and another swam up behind it.

"Shit," Meg cursed, claws extending. She growled, baring her teeth, and I watched as they sharpened and elongated into the perfect weapon for tearing.

The boat rocked to one side, then the other as the shapes positioned themselves underneath us.

"What are they doing?" she asked as the boat lurched upward.

The boat kept rising and my fears turned into elation. "They're rescuing us." Water was streaming out of the boat as the shapes raised us higher and higher. "This is Oceanus's work."

Two whales revealed themselves as their heads broke the surface, fully supporting our ship between them. Meg was gripping my arm tightly as she watched, her eyes wide, tears gathering and streaming down her cheeks as our rescuers began to swim forward, carrying us away from the monster-infested waters.

"I can't believe it," I heard her whisper.

The wind was whipping around us as the whales picked up speed, carrying us faster than any sail could have hoped to. I hugged her to me as we sat in the bow, watching the sea move quickly around us, the froth and spray whipping up.

The rain stopped, and the clouds were starting to break to reveal stars when the whales began to slow. The most dangerous areas were behind us, and the whales sank back into the water, leaving our ship to buoy on its own. We were sitting a little lower, water trapped in the hull, but that wouldn't be too difficult to remedy now that we were in steady seas.

"Thank you!" Meg called after the whales as they disappeared.

A surprised laugh burst from me, and she turned, a wry smile on her face. "What? I'm not sure how to speak whale, and I wanted to at least express our gratitude."

I pulled her in for a kiss, tasting the sea spray on her lips. "And I love that. I just wasn't expecting it."

We dried off as best we could and settled down together on the deck to rest, staring at the sky.

"You know, I spoke to Kronos through the Oracle. It certainly left an impression, felt like he actually cared, but I still didn't trust it. After this..."

My hands massaged her shoulders as she leaned against me. "It's acceptable to have doubts. They won't hold it against you," I said, smiling warmly. I had a suspicion that Kronos had said the same.

"I grew up believing they only intended to use me. When I spoke to Kronos—I almost felt like I was betraying myself. I'd hated them for so long, but now I was ready to believe in just one brief conversation that Kronos could be the father I never had? That I could have the family I was always so jealous of others for having?"

"So you fought harder against that feeling and doubled down on the idea that he was deceiving you." I finished her argument, one that I'd had before myself.

The wood under her feet scuffed as she toed at a crack in the board. "Like I'm already trying to convince myself that saving us was only so they didn't have to start over with another construct."

"That's a fair assessment," I admitted. Meg looked at me sharply and I cupped her cheek, my fingers tilting her chin toward me. "Fair, but incorrect. How much do you know about them?"

"Only what Gareth told me."

I gasped. "Gareth?"

She nodded. "Sorry. I think there's a lot for both of us to tell."

I listened intently as Meg relayed her story up until we'd met. I was shocked, horrified and angered at what Belsioch had made her suffer for his own selfish games. I could barely contain my anguish when she told me what happened to Arthur.

"There's still so much that I don't know. About them or myself," she confided. "And I'm terrified of making another mistake like I did with Gareth. Kronos told me to trust myself, but... that's easier said than done."

"Do you think that might be why you can't access your ability to travel?"

"No." She shook her head, but paused. "I don't know." She changed the subject. "What about you?"

I smiled. "What about me?"

"What's your story? How did you get on the wrong side of an Ætherim?"

"Ah." I paused, deciding on the best point of the story to start. "When the Titans threw me back in time, I landed in the North, in Viking territory. I couldn't stand the cold."

"Probably ruined your bronze tan," Megiste joked.

I gave her a sideways smile. She was odd and so easy-going. Not at all what I expected from a child of Titans, and it made me fall for her all the more.

I nodded. "That, and if I had to stomach fermented shark one more time, not even the promise of one day reuniting with my brothers would be enough to make it worth it."

When Meg laughed, I gave myself a moment to drink in the sound. "I worked my way back to the Aegean, providing security for merchant groups. It was where I was most comfortable. Maybe not the smartest choice given it would be a natural place to look for me if anyone was so inclined. But it was my homeland. I couldn't turn my back on it forever.

"When I reached Athens, I found the city was far different a couple hundred years prior to when I would have grown up here. I quickly endeared myself to the elites and the commanders of various military outfits. I had a lot of world experience for someone who looked so young.

"Meanwhile, I saw the conditions that the people were living in on the bottom tiers of society. People roved the streets every night to cause harm just for the sake of hurting people. There were no night watchmen, people would barricade themselves inside their homes when the sun went down. Fear was constant."

I looked at her. "Do you know what I am?"

She shook her head. "I noticed the fangs, but that's all." She smiled. "I don't want to assume."

I blew a curl out of my face. "My mother was Nosmortem."

Megiste stilled, her eyes roving over me. "Wow. I thought my lineage was notable, but you have an OG vampire for a mother?"

"OG?" I asked, not even a little familiar with the term.

She grinned. "Sorry. It means she's an original." She pushed away from me and sat up. "You said 'was'?"

"She was murdered. Retribution from my father."

"That's horrible."

"So was he." I moved on, not wanting to touch on that subject just yet. "I had a habit of roaming the streets at night, to hunt. I would only kill if I caught them in the act of something heinous. One night I came across a man disemboweling another, all for a few coins in his purse. He died, same as his victim. Turned out he was a favorite acolyte of Mithras."

"I'm a little familiar with him, but not much," she said.

"He's brutal, and vengeance is his specialty. The Romans had him as a favorite patron of their armies. And I'd met him before, in battle. Though, I was with the Titans at the time. He lost, and I'd inadvertently put myself back in his orbit."

I must have paused for too long because I felt Megiste's fingers twine into mine. I looked around at her, startled. "Oh."

"You don't have to tell me if you don't want to."

I shook my head. "It was a dark time, but it's mostly hard to tell because there are many things I don't remember."

She listened with absolute attention and no judgment. When I finished, she took my hand. "I'm sorry that happened."

I sighed. "It mostly just confirms the fact that we need to free the Titans so they can continue what they started and bring balance between the gods and everyone else."

"Is that really what they want?" asked Megiste. She wiped absently at a smudge of mud on her knee.

"Keeping the Ætherim from gathering too much power, yes." I laughed derisively. "We've all seen what they do with it."

She still looked bothered and I tilted her chin up to look at me. "Megiste."

"Meg," she said with a tight smile. "Just call me Meg."

I nodded. "Okay. What's bothering you?"

"What's going to happen. At the end of all this?"

I paused, lips parted in surprise. "What do you mean?"

"I'm a weapon, right? A tool? Even if I have a mind of my own, is that going to matter at the end? Or just make it more difficult to say goodbye?"

I inhaled, sharply. "Do you think their freedom means your death?"

She nodded. "Doesn't it? That's what I was always told."

I sat up and faced her, making sure she saw my earnestness. "I don't know what waits at the end, but I do know they wouldn't sacrifice you. They agonized over your creation. It wasn't lost on them that a construct's purpose precludes it from having any kind of free will, but they put it in the hands of the Fates and hoped they would step in. And they did. They made you whole and conscious and free." Her eyes darted to mine with such sudden hope it took my breath away. "There will still be danger and any one of us could be lost, but the ultimate goal is for you to join the Titans when they make their escape. To stand by their side. By all our sides."

She nodded and worried her lip with her teeth. The skin puckered and turned white and I ran my thumb along it, causing her to release it and stare up at me. Her lower lip was plump and moist, and my fingers moved to her throat, resting lightly against her pulse. My nostrils flared as I took in her scent, her arousal, and her gasp made my cock twitch.

Voice husky, I asked, "And what do you want, my Fated one?" I dipped my head and ran my lips along her jaw, fingers still splayed across her slender neck. My nails raked her artery, not breaking the skin, tracing the lifeline down to her clavicle.

She took in a ragged breath, her fingers wrapping in my hair with an eagerness that made me chuckle, low and dangerous.

"How will this work?"

That puzzled me. I raised my head. "Do you mean—?"

Another worried nibble of her lip and she pulled away, but I kept my grasp on her. It even surprised me, my reluctance to let her move even a few steps away.

"I didn't tell you something I should have," she said. She threw her hands up as she quickly clarified. "Not that it's anything dangerous or weird. Well, it is weird. Definitely weird."

"Meg," I said, gently. "Just tell me. I'm sure it's not that bad."

"I haven't always been able to shift into a wolf. When Gareth and I bonded—"

I could only stare in confusion until her words sank in. "You mean—"

She nodded.

"You took on his power?"

"Not all of it. I just... co-opted it? He didn't become any weaker. It didn't affect him at all, really. But his power coursed through me and stuck. I can even feel the wolf part of me, like she was awakened after being dormant all these years. Like she was always a part of me, I just never knew. As far as we can figure it's due to my being a construct. I'm kind of like an empty vessel that can take on whatever form or function it's given. This seems to be an interesting side effect."

I leaned against the mast in shock. "That's—"

"A lot to take in," she conceded. "I know. Since you're a vampire—"

"Part vampire. My father is a demon." One of the kings of hell, but that detail could wait. I shook my head. "I honestly have no idea how that would work. Shifters are possessed of an animal spirit around the time of birth. Sometimes they can be made, though, so that transfer of a spirit to you would still make sense. Vampires can be made or sired, so it would stand to reason that you would take on that ability."

"It seems like a lot of different powers to be present in one person," she said. "And not all of which would play nice."

"Unless the first mate you bonded with was the only time that transfer would occur." I laughed. "In which case, I'm sorry. You should've met Hadi. He's a dragon."

She only smiled and I continued. "But the demon part. You either are, or aren't. Demons must be born, by parentage." I scratched my chin thoughtfully, chafing at the stubble. I hated not being clean shaven. "But you were created by Titans, brought into being and made real by the Fates. I don't think we can say any of the rules apply for sure."

"I guess we'll just have to experiment and find out. If you're game?" asked Meg with a grin.

I growled and lunged toward her. Her delightful giggle turned into a moan as I claimed her lower lip in my teeth, lightly grazing the skin before running my tongue along it. My hands ran through her soft hair. Although we'd run from an army, escaped a city under siege, survived a gale that almost drowned us, and she'd been chasing my pathetic, cursed ass all over the city for days, her scent was intoxicating.

Her lips parted and my tongue swept through, tasting her. Her hands twisted in my clothes, pulling me closer and I picked her up, her thighs immediately squeezing on either side of me in a vise grip.

I inhaled a ragged breath when Meg rolled against my straining cock and I pinned her against the mast. I hastily undid the brooch at her shoulder and let her peplos fall to her waist, exposing taut pink nipples which I captured in my mouth.

Meg moaned and squirmed beneath me, bucking her hips. I trailed a line of kisses from her breasts to her throat. I licked and nipped the tender skin, my lips resting on her pulse once again.

My fangs had extended in my hunger and arousal, and I lightly scraped them against her neck. She gasped, hands grasping the back of my head, the feel of her nails trailing against my scalp driving me into a frenzy.

I lifted my head and looked to her for permission. Her eyes held no fear of me whatsoever. With the edge of one of my fangs, I cut the skin just next to her vein, only deep enough to draw a thin line of crimson to the surface. She moaned and bucked, her pulse quickening, and I ran my tongue along the line of blood.

A rumble of pleasure echoed from deep within my chest and my pupils dilated at the first taste. It was sweet and spicy and heady and *powerful*. I licked again, suckling at her throat, teasing more blood to the surface. When it ceased flowing, I reopened the cut, a little deeper this time.

Meg writhed, holding me close. I lapped at her neck, going slow, savoring the taste of her, the way the blood pounded as she neared climax.

I eased her to the ground, and she eagerly guided my hand to the apex of her thighs while pulling my mouth toward her neck once again. I latched on to her throat, still not using my teeth, and buried my fingers in her pussy, moaning into her neck as the slick, hot channel convulsed around my fingers. My thumb swirled around her clit, and she gasped while two fingers pumped into her. I added a third, pressing into her nub with the pad of my thumb.

"Oh, gods!" she gasped, bucking her hips. My cock was painfully eager to plunge into her, but I held off the urge by focusing on the sweet blood coating my mouth. I didn't want this encounter to be over quickly.

My fingers plunged faster and deeper and she cried out again, the first pulses of orgasm wracking her body. I licked along her throat and curved my fingers just right, the next two strokes taking her over the edge.

Her pussy spasmed around my fingers as she clung to me, moaning and gasping as the climax overtook her. Her cut healed, and I traced another line of kisses back to her breasts, teasing the hard buds of her nipples with my tongue, fingers still pumping as I brought her down slowly.

Meg was shivering and gasping for breath, her large, violet eyes fixing me with a still-hungry stare. I helped her sit up.

"What would you like to do next?" I asked.

# CHAPTER TWELVE

# Bel

"What's happening!" I roared, pummeling my fist into the wall. Dust and rock shattered, scattering on the ground. My nephilim "aides" were being their normal useless selves. Risha crouched in the corner, trying to support her twin. He looked a little less than well; I'd broken most of his body and blood was oozing in a steady flow around him.

Even with my shoulder stiff from that prick, Apollo's arrow, I was able to crush the pathetic excuse for a nephilim while Risha watched, helpless to stop me.

"It shouldn't be this difficult. She's not a mastermind and she's still confused and weak from her time spent in the cage. She's only got one of her paramours, maybe two by now, to keep her guarded. It's those weak creatures against ME! Their victories may be small, but it's still more than they should have had!" I rounded on Risha. "If you'd been doing your job properly!"

"Please, my lord! Just give me a chance to figure it out! I know I can!"

"You had your chance!" I bellowed. "You've had plenty of chances! Now that bitch is gaining allies among other Ætherim. They've allowed her to hide from me!" I stalked forward and pulled Risha away from her brother, throwing her toward her workstation. "Leave that pathetic creature to die and get back to work!"

I motioned to two other nephilim, part of the cadre that I'd called in to help. Since there was no need to hide my deeds from Meg anymore, I'd brought in all the cavalry to operate in the open. The lodge was now a buzzing center of planning, our home base from which we would stage our final war against the Titans and everyone that stood with them.

I'd destroy them all, and make Meg watch while I bathed in their blood. My hands clenched the air as I felt them twisting around her neck until she tuned purple. When everyone she ever cared for was dead, then I would allow her to follow.

The nephilim, I still had no idea what their names were, nor did I care, picked up Ursal and dragged him away. Risha extended her hand, sobbing as she watched him get tossed in a corner.

I narrowed my eyes at her. "What did I tell you?"

Risha snapped her focus back to me and stifled her cries, shuffling through the papers and books at her station. I curled my lip in disgust. She was too frazzled to think straight. I wouldn't be getting anything useful from her for some time.

I patrolled down the lines of desks and the various creatures that sat behind them, watching their progress as they also sought for answers to the serious problem that Meg was becoming.

"My lord, you asked to see us?" Hypnos stood before me, his whelp in tow. Morpheus couldn't even meet my eyes.

And they called themselves my brethren? What a joke.

"The job that I set you wasn't a hard one, was it?" My voice was dangerously quiet, and they fidgeted, trying to work out where this conversation was going before I got there. Trying to prepare themselves for the fallout.

It wouldn't save them from my wrath.

"No, my lord. It wasn't. We were just—"

"I don't care what 'you were just'!" I screamed. "You had one job! You failed!"

"We can try again. We lost her in the melee when Xerxes attacked, but—"

I cut my hand in a severe motion to silence them. "The moment she leaves Greece, you're worthless to me."

"That's not quite true, my lord," ventured Hypnos. "If we figure out what time period she landed in, we can rejoin our timelines in Greece and travel overland to find her."

I didn't think my disgust could've been greater, but apparently... "Why would you waste your time, and mine, on that ridiculous notion? Why would I not send someone else that wouldn't have to traverse—the goddamn—globe!" I punctuated each pause between words with a clap of my hands.

A thought came so suddenly then, I couldn't believe I hadn't thought of it before. I shoved past Hypnos and flung the door to the torture room open. I had the bitch's blood everywhere. Why had I wasted my time with bringing in Ætherim long weakened by their own reticence and apathy?

I needed to bring in the best. Beings that couldn't fail, that were utterly unstoppable.

Now all I needed to do was remember how to call them. I'd never met them, only heard of them in passing, never imagining

I'd need to make use of their services. That gave me pause. Would I be admitting my own failures?

I spat. It would be a failure not to destroy Meg and her *mates* as soon as possible.

To hell with it. I retreated within my own mind, digging deep to find the link I'd forged with Zader when I'd first appointed him chief torturer of the Titans. I'd wanted to make sure that in a pinch, I could send a message to destroy them all if there was any hope of one of their plans for escape actually working. Or, on the off chance that they escaped their individual prisons and Zader couldn't keep them in check, he would be able to reach me for help.

I felt the piqued interest and slow recognition as Zader felt my attempts to contact him. I don't think we'd ever spoken this way, so it was an unfamiliar experience.

*My lord,* he answered. *Is something wrong?*

*So many things,* I said, a bitter sneer twisting my mouth, *but that isn't important. I need to contact the Hounds. Do you know how I might go about it?*

*The Hounds? May I ask why?*

*That's of no concern.* It rankled me that my subordinate felt the need to question my actions.

*I meant no offense, my lord. I was curious whether I could be of service. It gets rather boring around here at times.*

*Do you know how to contact them or not?*

*Yes, my lord.* Pictures flooded my mind, the process laid out that would bring the Hounds to heel.

*Thank you, Zader. And you have my permission to make your work with the Titans as interesting as you'd like.*

*Thank you, my lord.*

The connection dropped, and I bustled back out into the main room, heading straight for the summoning circle Risha kept etched into the concrete.

"Is there something we can assist you with?" asked Hypnos, standing nervously by and watching my flurry of activity.

"You can shut up. Get out of my sight." I turned on the entire room at large and swept my arms, the sleeves of my robes billowing. "Everybody get out!"

Nobody attempted to argue. They all filed out of the basement and left me to the work. I stared down at the circle and pursed my lips, grabbing a piece of chalk and sketching out the symbols I'd seen in Zader's instruction. I grabbed a scalpel from a nearby workstation and slit my hand open, dripping blood into the center of the circle and drawing my power around me as I prepared to give the commands.

"Exter, Tarshi, Yarris." I called their names, forcing my will upon them to appear. "Show yourselves. Appear to me here, now. I call upon you, Exter, Tarshi, Yarris! Appear before me now!"

I continued to invoke them until a slight crackling noise entered my consciousness. The air inside the circle grew hazy, wavering like hot air swimming on the blacktop in the middle of summer. Three figures appeared, standing side by side, becoming clearer with each passing second.

There was a snapping sound, and they were suddenly fully manifested, real and deadly and smiling at me with unnerving, too-wide mouths. There were two men and a woman. The men had black three-piece suits and bowler hats, and the woman was wearing the same thing, just a pencil skirt instead of pants. Sleek black hair, oiled back, and in the woman's case, tied into a bun. It contrasted with their paper white skin, the blue veins running along their temples and in a network of spidery threads down their necks, disappearing into their starched shirt collars and standing out starkly.

"Belsioch," they said in unison. A chill ran down my spine. I'd faced creatures of all sorts, but never ones such as these. With a sudden jolt, I realized that if they broke through that circle, they could very well kill me. It would be a close match, in any case.

"Hounds," I acknowledged. "I've got a job for you."

All three of them, again in unison, dropped their heads to the side, their ears almost touching their shoulders. Those grins never leaving their faces. The black holes they had for eyes were limitless. If I stared into them for long enough, I had no doubt I'd be driven mad. Rumors always said their eyes reached the edge of the universe and held all the secrets of it. These creatures were almost as old as the world. Some say they were here first. They allowed us to populate this place because it gave them sustenance that was more fun to eat than stars and dark matter. Stars don't run and scream.

As I considered them, they must've been able to tell the path of my thoughts. Rumbling growls took the shape of laughter, a sound that would've been more at home in the body of Godzilla than these average humanoid vessels before me.

"Your fear is delicious," they said. Their heads snapped upright with a jolt, and I stumbled back a step. They lunged to the edge of the circle, their hands transforming into claws and raking against the barrier.

Fury rose to replace the fear. "You dare threaten me?" I asked, stepping forward and battering the barrier with my own power.

They hissed, their teeth momentarily becoming long, needlelike spears. I was reminded of the jaws of a lantern fish before they pasted their human faces back on and stepped into the center of the circle.

"What are you offering us for this job?" asked the man on the right.

I faltered. "What do you want?"

They smiled, and the woman stepped forward, hands clasped behind her back. "An admission."

I narrowed my eyes. "Of what?"

"You fears. Your failures. Your real reasons for wanting the girl and her mates dead."

Another stab of unease went through me. I hadn't told them what I wanted them to do.

"You didn't have to," said the woman, responding to my unspoken thoughts.

"If you can read my mind, why do you need me to say anything out loud?"

They smiled and spoke in unison. "Because it will cause you pain."

My fists clenched. These abominations thought they could mock me like this and get away with it?

"You are unable to retaliate against us, Belsioch. I wouldn't recommend it."

My lip curled. "Fine. I can't get to Megiste myself, so I need you to do it for me. Destroy her so thoroughly they won't be able to resurrect a thing."

They all stood there and blinked at me. "Fine! I can't accept a loss of any kind to the Titans. I want them gone! I hate them for what they've done."

"What have they done?" Asked the man on the left.

"They second guessed me! They tried to usurp me! My power is supreme, even among my kind! How dare they!"

More stupid blinking over their empty black eyes. I lunged forward. "I should rip your faces off your skulls."

"Clearly you don't want our help." They began to fade.

"Wait. I didn't release you."

"We came here of our own volition. The summoning makes people feel like they have a modicum of control. Keeps them from becoming blubbering idiots when their fear takes over."

"I'll give you anything else," I said.

They shrugged. "We don't want anything else."

I thought fast. "Not even Death?"

They paused.

"I could deliver him right to you, weakened. You could resolve all your quarrels."

"It is not... a disagreeable offer," said the woman.

"Then take it. And hunt down Megiste and her paramours. Kill them all. Leave nothing behind. Consume their souls, or whatever it is you do."

"A gross misunderstanding of how we operate, but alright." She tapped a boney finger to her chin. "Do you have a scent for us to follow?"

Shit. I'd forgotten to grab a rag or something else with Meg's blood on it. I glanced back at the torture room. Would that barrier break when I tossed it to them?

They smiled their unnerving smiles and stepped forward out of the circle, the barrier shattering with a horrible screech.

The man on the right spoke. "Like we said, we came here of our own volition. Your circle was never going to protect you."

"Wait." They stopped. "On second thought..."

They waited impatiently. "Yes?"

I licked my lips. "Don't kill them. Capture them. Bring them all to me."

The female pointed to the door. "We'll help ourselves."

I nodded and stepped back, feeling a creeping cold sweep over me that made me break out in chills as they passed. It was the aching cold of the vacuum of space. They disappeared into the torture room and closed the door behind them.

Minutes passed, then almost an hour. I heard nothing from inside the room, but that wasn't surprising. It was lined with iron and padded with soundproof material.

I crept forward and opened the door. It was empty. They'd disappeared from a chamber designed to prevent just that.

My hands trembled with an inkling of fear as I scanned every inch of the basement for their presence and I angrily clenched fists at my sides. Angry at myself, angry at them for their mockery.

I stalked over to the circle and brushed the chalk into smears, blowing out the candles and wiping at the blood before deciding to leave it to be someone else's problem.

In the meantime...

Upstairs and outside the various nephilim I'd called to my side were milling around, waiting for their orders. I saw that they'd deposited Ursal on the couch when I'd kicked them all out. He was getting blood everywhere and still stubbornly breathing. Risha tended to him and tried to clean up his wounds. There was a subtle healing energy coming from her as she used what rudimentary magick she possessed.

I resisted the urge to demand Ursal be taken outside, perhaps on the very couch on which he lay. Maybe they should light it on fire, just to hasten the process of his end. But no.

A nephilim noticed I'd come upstairs and snapped to attention. In a wave of motion, the others noticed and did the same. One of the females by the window motioned for the ones outdoors to come in, and they scrambled to do so. I noticed Hypnos and Morpheus were nowhere to be found. Running would only delay their punishment.

My troops lined up and waited for their orders, just like the old days. When the world was consumed in a fire and doused in the blood of mortals and Strangers as we fought for supremacy, to remake the world as it should have always been. With me on the throne, my followers at my side, and everyone else bowing before me.

The rest could and would die screaming. A small smile played on my lips at the thought. That will be a beautiful day, and long in coming.

"I've resolved the problem of the hunt for Megiste and the Desma. The Hounds are taking care of it."

There was a murmur, a mixture of shock and horror as the name of those monsters spread through the group. They had every right to be horrified.

"Now we need to work on another problem," I continued. I looked at Risha and she stood, a small moan escaping her brother's mouth as her healing energy was pulled away from him.

"What do you need from me, my lord."

I smiled. Much better.

"We need to find a way to move people through time. A lot of them. I want permanent, programmable gates made."

Another murmur, this time of incredulity. "I know it's never been done and the only theories that exist about it are written by madmen, or those that went mad shortly thereafter.

But we need to be ready on all fronts. I want to move at least three of you at any given time, to any given place. I trust the Hounds to do their job. Now I'm placing my attention on a special prize."

I let my gaze travel over my agents of chaos, meeting each of their eyes and waiting for that subtle nod or silent affirmation that they would follow me before moving on to the next.

Risha approached me tentatively. "My lord." She was fidgeting nervously with something on a chain around her neck, the shape of which was just visible beneath her shirt. She kept shooting pained glances at her brother and chewing on her lip. "I may have already solved the problem."

# CHAPTER THIRTEEN

# Meg

"What would you like to do next?"

Those words zinged through me, the wetness between my thighs redoubling. I licked my lips and my hand went tentatively to my neck. There was a thin pucker where the cut had been. The feel of his mouth latched onto my throat was intoxicating in a way I'd never imagined. I'd known some vampires, had seen them feed before, but until I'd experienced it firsthand, I'd had no idea how intense it was. And he hadn't even bitten me yet.

I let my peplos drop to the ground and stepped out of it, inviting him to do the same.

I'd noted how lean he was before, but now that I got the full sense of him, the muscles in his body were corded and deadly looking, like one of the big cats. The build of someone who could move fast and with such grace that you wouldn't know what hit you until it was too late.

Where Gareth was cut like a professional body builder, Andrus was softer. There was definition, but not the severe V-shape that pointed an arrow straight to his dick.

I leaned back against the mast again, enjoying being out in the open under the night sky, stretching my arms up over my head. As Andrus stalked closer, I hooked my knee around his hip, wrapping my leg tight around his waist.

He ran his hands over my body, caressing my thighs, fingertips grazing my apex, still sensitive enough to elicit a gasp. He lined up at my entrance and hooked my other leg around his waist. Then his hands continued over the globes of my ass, up my waist and skimmed my breasts before trailing all the way up my arms, where he clasped his hands in mine.

His face was an inch from mine and he stared into my eyes, pushing inside me torturously slow. My head eased back and my eyes closed, but he stopped. I opened my eyes and looked at him, and he continued without a word, a small smile on his face. His hands clasped tighter on mine, fingers threading through my own.

In one steady thrust, his hips bumped against me and I groaned. His cock was thinner, but long, and was hitting spots inside me that had never been touched. The waves gently rocked us back and forth, the water a little choppier now.

Andrus dipped his head to my neck and his fangs teased goosebumps across my flesh. He pulled out and glided back in, building momentum.

A teasing of breath as he exhaled was all the warning before his fangs pierced my neck. Only a fraction of a second of pain before bliss took over. Without any buildup, I came, the sheer magick of the bite bringing me to climax. I cried out and squeezed my legs tighter around him, his movements becoming more frantic as he drove me wild on multiple fronts. My pussy clenched around him, resisting every time he pulled away.

The small movements of my hips I could make in this position added more delicious friction, while tingles of electric heat radiated from my throat. His tongue teased and soothed as he drank me in. Another wave of climax rolled over me and I screamed at the intensity, the sound carried away across the water.

I could feel his body tense as his own climax neared. He lifted his head, only a small smear of blood on his mouth, and I noticed his eyes were rimmed with dark red around the irises and his pupils had expanded, a black hole rimmed with red surrounded by an ocean of clear white sclera.

He kissed me deeply, and I tangled my tongue with his, the coppery aftertaste sending another shock wave of pleasure through me. Andrus growled, resting his forehead against mine as he gave one last thrust and came, filling me.

We stayed like that until our shaking stopped and our breathing steadied. I unwrapped my legs, and we separated, both of us sinking down onto the boards with wobbly knees.

Once I'd got my senses under control, I realized with disappointment that I felt the same. The rush, the magick, the crazy rainbow eyes. None of that happened.

"Do you feel any different?" I asked Andrus.

He shook his head, scooting closer to me and wrapping me in his arms. "No."

My face fell.

"It's alright. We're still mates. Gareth must be the only true-mate. Or he was just the first."

The last was added with a note of jealousy. So much for everyone playing nice in the bedroom. But I couldn't deny I was a little bitter myself. Once I'd felt that closeness with Gareth, I wanted it again, with all my mates. Maybe I was getting a little greedy, but I think Gareth would agree it's a hell of an experience to miss out on.

"I really wanted to share that with you." I felt like it was my fault, even though I knew that wasn't true. It was just another quirk of my magick that no one ever gave me the user manual for.

The seas had gone smooth after we'd finished our... exercise... but now they were getting choppy again. I looked at the mast. The sail had been lowered during the storm, but there was no movement in the fabric at all.

"Andrus?"

He'd been dozing with his head buried in my neck, but he stirred at the worry in my voice. "What's happened?"

"We're rocking an awful lot for there not to be any wind creating surf, right?"

His eyes narrowed at the sail and he stood, looking out over the railing. "The water is calm not a hundred yards away."

"Are the whales back?" I asked, afraid to think of the alternative.

Andrus leaned over the railing and sprang back as a giant serpentine tail whipped out of the water, lashing at the empty air where Andrus had been standing. It wrapped around the railing and crushed it, pulling it away from the ship with a horrible crack.

The tail, lined with scales, the water cascading off it as it rose from the water once again, lashed across the entire width of the deck and pulled. The boat dipped and I grabbed at the mast, trying to keep myself from sliding toward it.

"Meg!" Andrus yelled, tossing me a rope that he secured around the rudder. I grabbed it and pulled myself away from the creature, frantic as the rest of it appeared from the depths.

Too many teeth. That was the first and only thing I noticed before Andrus grabbed hold of the sword he'd tied down to keep it from washing away in the gale and charged at the monster.

The tail was as wide as he was tall, but he did a good amount of damage to it with a few strikes of the blade. The monster shrieked and released the ship, smashing its tail down on the stern, which sent the boat bobbing violently and threw me to the side.

Andrus was crouched and waiting for the creature to strike. The tail struck out at him and he dodged it, finding the wound he'd already dealt it and landing a few more strikes. He'd almost cut it halfway through, bone and viscera glistening as blood spattered thickly over the deck.

It swiped again and Andrus ducked, throwing himself forward to pop up on the opposite side, hacking away. A sound I could only equate to an animal carcass being butchered made my stomach roll, made worse by the thrashing of the ship in the water. Meaty, wet sounds combined with slicing and the spatter of gore.

Andrus raised his arms high to take a final swing that would sever the beast's tail, but the slick blood all over the deck cost him his footing. He fell hard and before I could react, the tail had wrapped tightly around him and dragged him over the edge to disappear into the water.

"Andrus!" I screamed, scrabbling for the edge. In a matter of seconds, the water had stilled and the only evidence that the monster had been there at all was a haze of blood on the surface.

I sat in the bow of the boat for what felt like hours, huddled against the incoming rain clouds. The wind had turned bitter and cold as it shrieked across the water, catching in the many holes all over the ship and rumbling underneath the deck.

The first time it happened, I thought the monster was back for the rest of its meal. I couldn't stop crying. I kept reaching out for anything familiar, mostly my mates, hoping that maybe I could get a lock on them since we were out in the middle of the ocean with no interference. Maybe Andrus wasn't dead, maybe the monster had just carried him off. He was part vampire, so maybe he didn't need as much air as regular people, or maybe it would keep him safe against the creature and allow him to escape.

But then more despair would overcome me when I realized all those things were just fantasies. I couldn't sense even a trace of him, and the more time went on... he wasn't coming back. I sent my own desperate plea to Oceanus, hoping he could intercede, but there was nothing.

The ship was sitting even lower in the water now, with the additional damage the serpent had dealt. I couldn't go below deck to stay out of the storm. It was too flooded, and if that continued, I didn't want to be stuck in there if the ship went down. Not that it mattered.

A little searching discovered a tarp of oilskin in the bottom of a chest that was nailed to the deck. It smelled rancid, but I crawled under it anyway once the thin fabric of my peplos no longer kept me from shivering.

I pulled the skin over my head as the rain fell harder and curled up into the fetal position, trying to lull myself to sleep. I'd debated raising the sail and seeing if the wind would blow me toward land. The Aegean was full of islands and the mainland surrounded most of it, so the likelihood was pretty good.

Gods knew I had no hope of navigating, so I'd be completely at the whim of the tides. But I couldn't do it. Part of me didn't want to give up hope Andrus would find his way back.

My eyelids were too heavy for my fear to keep them open anymore, and I drifted to sleep.

I found myself in a gray landscape that I recognized as the purgatory outside of time. My heart leaped, but when I reached for my magick, it still didn't respond.

"This is a dream. It was the only way I could reach you."

I spun and threw myself at Gareth, but his form dissipated and only became solid again once I'd passed through his body.

"I'm sorry, we're only projections," he said sadly. "I'd wrap you tight in my arms if I could." He looked stricken. "I can feel your pain."

"I lost him, Gareth. Andrus is dead. That sea monster just grabbed him and there was nothing I could do." I hyperventilated and Gareth stood as close as he could, his hands hovering over my shoulders to provide what comfort he was able. "I got you stuck someplace and I can't find you. I sent Arthur to his death and Andrus was snatched up by a monster." My voice grew shrill. "I've lost all of you and I can't access my magick! What am I supposed to do!"

Gareth made a soothing humming sound. "Gods I wish I could hold you. You shouldn't be going through this alone."

"Where are you?" I asked. "Is it a place or somewhere between?"

Gareth shook his head. "It must be somewhere between because it's mostly just an empty landscape. I'm not sure what to make of it, and there aren't any landmarks of note to give a hint. I am fine, lass. There's no danger here."

A nagging feeling of distrust bloomed in my gut. "How do I know this isn't another trick by Morpheus?"

He smiled. "I don't know how to convince you that it's really me, we don't know a whole lot about each other yet. Except maybe that your eyes flashed like rainbows when we bonded."

Relief was heady as I fought the urge to launch myself into his arms again. It had to be him. "So what should I do?"

"You said it was Andrus?"

I nodded, and he looked relieved.

"Have hope. Andrus is a very hard man to kill."

My heart leaped to my throat. "You know he's alive?"

He shook his head again. "Not for sure, and I'll never forgive myself if I'm giving you false hope when you're hurting. Andrus's heritage makes him strong in ways we can't comprehend. He survives things most Strangers wouldn't, including regenerating lost limbs. I've seen amazing feats from him. If anyone could survive this, it's him. Just give it more time."

"Why am I still cut off from my magick?"

"That I don't know. Are you sure it's not self-inflicted? All the stress you're under would put most people out of their minds by now. There has to be side effects." He raised his hand and ran the backs of his fingers a fraction away from my cheek. "Give yourself some grace. You're already carrying so much. The magick will return when it knows it won't destroy you."

"Destroy me?"

"In a manner of speaking." He smiled. "You're not delicate by any means, but if you could use your magick right now, what do you think you would be doing?"

I bowed my head. "Something self-destructive. Like charging headlong at the enemy."

His eyes held all the warmth and love that I so desperately needed right now, and my heart ached that he wasn't truly with me.

"I have complete faith that this will all work out. You'll find a way."

"That's a lot of confidence I'm not sure is deserved."

"But it is. I know you'll find me. You've already done it twice. Third time's the charm."

He bent his head and leaned close for a kiss. For the fraction of a second before our bodies dissipated, our lips met, and it sent a revitalized energy through my whole body.

I woke, gasping for breath. My hand shot to my lips, the tingle of that electric encounter still present. I could even smell the earthy musk of his scent lingering on me. That encounter was genuine.

The pattering of the rain against the oilskin had ceased, and I'd slept the whole night through. Dawn was breaking, clear and vibrant.

And I realized with a jolt that I'd drifted quite a way from our original landing spot. The rocky outcrop I'd seen in the distance was nowhere in sight. Open water surrounded me.

Even if Andrus was alive, how would he find me? My mind spiraled in a panic, but I stopped and took a breath. Panicking wouldn't do me any good, nor would feeling sorry for myself.

I breathed deeply, trying to think of a solution. The calls of the whales came to mind, along with an idea so crazy it just might work.

Summoning up all things Andrus, his touch, his scent, the taste of him, along with his signature, I allowed myself to sink deep into those memories, and the excitement of our time together.

I let the energy flow through me until I could feel it like a palpable thing, writhing to get loose with a mind of its own. With only a slight bit of trepidation, given what horrors had recently come out of the water, I leaned over the edge of the boat and put my hands on the surface, channeling that energy into a torpedo that I set loose in one big burst.

My call for Andrus rolled over the water. *Come and find me.*

Please, gods, let him find me.

# Chapter Fourteen

# Meg

It was almost noon. I was sitting in meditation, both to keep myself calm and to internalize the confidence Gareth had in me. It felt like an impossible task, something that I wouldn't have a hope of living up to.

I wasn't exactly a fuckup, but I'd made a lot of mistakes, especially in the last month. Maybe I should forgive myself for some of it, but it was still hard to stomach.

A self-imposed block on my power made us vulnerable. I could've moved us on to some place safe, somewhere not besieged by an entire army set on razing one of the greatest cities the ancient world had ever known. I could've gotten Gareth back already, and we'd be on our way to the next Desma, and the next.

If I was stronger. If I didn't have so many doubts. No matter how hard I tried to push those thoughts away, they just kept swimming up, ugly and mean. Screaming my failures in my face as they laughed with bloody teeth. All... my... fault.

Yes, it was my *destiny* to do these things. But it didn't make it easier. It only made every misstep harder to swallow.

And I didn't know what to do with these feelings, either. Everything I'd been so sure of had turned out to be wrong. My heart and instincts said I was in the right place, but my head was still fighting to hate the Titans at all costs. Kronos had shown what I could only describe as fatherly love. Not that I was an expert in it, but I could feel the difference. That tender care as he looked at me from the Oracle's eyes. The pride. The sadness when I told him I didn't trust him, and the acceptance of the fact. It didn't throw him into a rage, only made him feel pain that he'd failed me.

Until my mates, if someone moved to protect me, it was for their own gain only. I was always a pawn in someone else's game. But those were the actions of individuals. The Titans sent me to the wrong keepers, but they didn't do it on purpose.

My concentration broke. I rubbed my hands over my face in frustration. Another doom spiral, dragging me down into the infinite possibilities of what my life could have been if only I hadn't been surrounded by shitty people.

"But you were. It happened, it's over, there's nothing you can do to change it," I mumbled into my hands, still clasped firmly over my face. "All you can do is put your big girl panties on and get on with your life. The best revenge on all of them will be to show them that they didn't destroy you. Show them how strong you are."

"I don't know exactly what you're talking about, but I agree with the sentiment."

I dropped my hands, resisting a small shriek of surprise. Andrus was crouched in front of me, water streaming from his hair, healing wounds all over his body, relief and happiness in his eyes.

Tears were already streaming down my face as I threw myself at him, and we toppled to the deck. He grunted in pain, and I hastily tried to backpedal, but he held me close.

"I'm alright," he said, burying his face in my hair. "I'm alright."

I pulled away enough to clasp my hands on either side of his face and really get a look at him. "What happened?"

He shook his head. "I couldn't really tell you. It was just a flurry of fighting and stabbing. The beast could clearly inflict damage of his own." He looked down at his body and I watched, mesmerized, as a wound on his chest sealed shut in front of my eyes.

I ran my fingers over the puckered scar. "That must've been a helluva wound to just be finishing healing."

A strange look came over his face, a quirk of the mouth that wasn't quite a smile. "One benefit of being what I am. If I come close enough to death but I manage to escape to a place of safety where I can heal, my body will shut down all unnecessary function to do so. It would look like death to anyone that didn't know better, but my body would be slowly repairing itself. I've woken up in a grave more than once."

"That's what Gareth meant."

Andrus inhaled sharply and looked around. "You've spoken to him? Is he here?"

"No. Sorry, I didn't mean to get your hopes up. He found me in a dream, in the space between time."

Andrus smoothed the hair back from my face. "Any luck with tapping into your magick?"

"No. But once you're healed, I think I might know a way to make it happen."

I explained how Gareth had bolstered my power. "Even if we didn't bond in the same way, I think we can use our connection to jump start the process."

"Where will we go?"

The first hints of apprehension appeared in Andrus's previously unwavering confidence.

"How long has it been since you've left the Aegean?"

He laughed darkly. "I've watched Crete rise and fall, the city-states clash time and time again, the Hittites, the Egyptians, the Persians, the Gauls... thousands of years."

"Were you always a soldier?"

"I tried to be a priest of Poseidon, but I couldn't bear the monotony. I took the path of a merchant for a while, made a decent living, but when that became boring, I set out to find new trade avenues, discover new resources. Made a killing with that because I already knew where to look, but that also took the fun out of it. I ended up becoming a pirate for a short time, which was a lively affair."

"A pirate?"

He shot me a crooked grin. "A scourge of the seas. But yes, I ultimately gravitated back to military life, no matter what. It gave me a clear-cut purpose. And now my ultimate purpose has arrived." He wrapped his arms around me, and I leaned my back against his chest, careful not to rest too much weight on him.

"I will keep you safe, always." His breath tickled my scalp as he placed a kiss on the crown of my head. "And I will always find my way back to you."

I traced my fingers along his arms. "When I thought you'd died—"

His arms squeezed tighter. "I'm sorry you had to endure that alone."

"That's when Gareth found me. I'd lost all hope, but he told me he believed you were still alive." I craned my head around to look him in the eye. "These—potent—emotions are still so odd to me. It doesn't make sense that I can be so attached to someone I just met, but this is the second time it's happened, and it only reinforces that the things I'm feeling are true." I raised a hand and cupped his cheek.

Andrus smiled and leaned in to kiss me, his lips still tasting of salt. It was tender and unhurried, and we parted with the sheepish grins of young lovers.

"Tell me more about your life," I said, snuggling back against him.

"What would you like to know?"

I thought for a minute. "Where did you grow up?"

"Back then it was called Babylon."

My ears perked up.

"My mother was Nosmortem, as I already mentioned. My father was a demon lord who'd taken a liking to the earthly realm and relocated his stronghold to Babylon in its later years. Have you heard of the Hanging Gardens?"

I balked, eyes wide "Yeah. They were real?"

There was an edge to his voice as he continued, the subject of his father clearly a sore one. "He built them. For my mother. He treated her like a queen until she gave him a son. When he'd gotten what he wanted, he sent her away. I was only a small boy. He made hell on earth, and forced me to call it home until I was old enough to run and stay gone."

"I'm so sorry. Did you ever find your mother again?"

Andrus hummed. "Yes. But I wish I hadn't. She was already broken, and seeing me again only brought her more pain. She tried to welcome me into the life she'd rebuilt for herself in Macedonia, but she had a new family by then. So I left. Wandered for a long time until I settled in the Aegean and made a new life I could call my own."

"Clearly I have a knack for picking painful subjects. You don't have to talk about this if you don't want to," I said.

He tucked my head under his chin. "It's actually a relief to share it. It's been a long time since I've felt comfortable enough to talk about my past.

"At some point I joined up with a military outfit and they accepted me into their ranks without hesitation. There wasn't a lot of action, we were mostly auxiliary. Brought in only when minor skirmishes became a little more than."

I could feel the tension building in his body and the muscles in his arms corded as they tightened around me.

"One day we were visited by two men who looked like soldiers. Young, powerful warriors, that were extremely skilled in combat. They were with our outfit for a couple of days before anyone started asking questions about them. They kept to themselves mostly, you see. Nobody complained about their presence because of their skill, but we knew absolutely nothing about them. They barely spoke unless they were spoken to first."

"Unnerving," I said.

He nodded and his chest rumbled with a sound of agreement. "Then things began to get strange. People from the villages started flocking to these men, the other soldiers in the outfit were inseparable from them. It seemed like everyone was being lured in by some kind of spell. And still in the middle of it all, these two men didn't do anything different. They stood in the middle of their devotees, still barely speaking, but looking more and more... powerful. They began to exude authority. And I swear there was an aura of glowing light building around them little by little. And every one of their followers—worshipers—were getting weaker. Aging before my eyes."

"You were the only one unaffected?" I asked.

"It seemed that way. There were other Strangers in the outfit, but they seemed even more drawn in than the humans. Once I felt something was truly wrong, I tried to blend into the background, to avoid drawing their notice." He placed another absentminded kiss on top of my head. "Although I'm not sure if they really cared either way. What was one man going to do, even if he did see what was happening?"

"So what did you do?"

"The decline began to hasten. Friends that had appeared just a bit older and tired, the next day appeared like they'd aged thirty years. There was no doubt in my mind that those 'men' intended to drain them of every drop of life force they had. And the people wouldn't even realize because they were too busy prostrating themselves in front of their new gods."

"Who were they?" I asked, almost breathless.

He exhaled a sharp breath of air through his nose. "They were far from *new* gods."

My eyes widened and my hand wrapped around his arm.

"Romulus and Remus. This was just around the time of Etruria's decline, and Rome's rise."

"Oh, shit."

He nodded. "Of course, I didn't discover this until I'd challenged them. I walked past their throngs of devotees, dying at their feet, to the two shining gods seated in the middle of them, smug as you please. They looked at me like I was nothing more than a cockroach as I approached them. Their eyes barely even focused on me when I began to rail against them, calling on them to stop this, trying to rally whatever senses the people had left. But it was too late to get through to any of them. And the gods simply stared ahead with smug smiles of satisfaction."

"And then?"

Another burst of air as he laughed. "I didn't realize I told such a compelling story."

"Don't sell yourself short. And then?" I prompted.

"I drew my sword and cut off one of their heads."

"You what!"

"That's about the reaction Remus had as his brother's head hit the ground, only of shock and anger instead of surprise. I should've taken a bigger swing and aimed for both their heads at once."

"But it wouldn't have killed them."

"No," he agreed. "But it would've given me a little more time to figure out how to do that. As it was, Remus immediately engaged me in battle. When his brother regathered himself, it was two against one. I'm difficult to tire out, but they were quickly wearing me down."

He paused, and I squirmed around so I could look at him. He was staring at the deck, brow furrowed before his eyes met mine, and he smiled. "Then he appeared."

Instead of prompting with a question, I frowned and pinched his thigh at his teasing, and he laughed.

"Kronos himself."

I'd guessed the answer, but it still elicited a gasp.

"The most regal-looking man I'd ever seen had come upon the battle. He was a giant, his beard was styled like royalty, and his robes were the deepest indigo. I wasn't sure how long he'd been there before I noticed him, but once I did, he laughed and clapped his hands. The twins stopped in their attacks, and I sank to my knees with exhaustion."

"What did the twins think of the new arrival?" I asked, picturing how intimidating it would have been to see a man such as that appear seemingly out of nowhere. And to have him watch a fight to the death like it was grand entertainment.

"They actually looked afraid. And I couldn't figure out why. This man was clearly powerful, but they were gods."

"Kronos disguised his power that well?"

Andrus shook his head. "I think I didn't realize it because of how different his signature was from the Ætherim."

"Is it really?" I asked. How had I not noticed?

"Very much. You might share in their signature, but until you've met them in person... it's not something that's easy to explain. But they are undeniably *other*."

I settled back into his arms for the rest of the story, his cooler-than-average body a nice counter to the sun as the day grew hot. "Hey," I said, a sudden epiphany hitting me. "How are you sitting in the sun? Doesn't it hurt?"

"No. It's not comfortable, and my eyes tire quickly, but I can tolerate it."

"Is that why you always wore the cloak?" I asked.

He nodded. "That, I wanted to hide myself away." We let that sit for a moment before he continued. "Kronos held up a hand and the twins froze. 'You have grossly abused your power here,' he'd said. The twins tried to give him an explanation, but he wouldn't hear it. 'Will you give back what you stole?' he asked them. But they swore they couldn't, what was done, was done. So Kronos nodded his head thoughtfully and paced a couple of times while he made a decision. Then he raised a hand again and the gods just…"

Andrus made a motion with his hands, exploding them outward. "Unraveled. Into a million threads. The air filled with the smell of blood, and I could feel a fine mist of it on my face and arms. Then I realized who this man must be. Or *what* he must be. Only a god can kill a god."

# CHAPTER FIFTEEN

# *Andrus*

Meg's eyes were wide as she was remembering something of her own. "Had you met many beings that powerful before? How did you not freak out? The first time I met Bel"—I winced as she said his name so casually—"I could barely stop the shaking. I cried, it was just so overwhelming."

"Once I realized what I was looking at, I was too numb to do much more than stare. I'd just fought against two gods, this was just another rung on the ladder of impossible occurrences that day."

"And your only option is to go up that ladder because below you is a sea of doubt... and maybe piranhas," she said.

I laughed. "That's kind of what I was thinking, yes. How much worse could it be if I kept climbing? This man didn't seem like he wanted to hurt me. On the contrary." My voice got soft. That day was still crystal clear in my mind and I relived the emotions as if they were fresh. "He looked at me like I was... real. Most beings I'd met that were anywhere near that powerful, especially the ones I'd just fought, looked past me or through me like I was less than. Or not even there at all. But it felt like he saw me. And actually gave a damn."

Meg hummed thoughtfully. I imagined it would have been a lot like that for her when she'd met Kronos through the Oracle.

"He stepped forward and put out his hand, like he was greeting a person of equal rank. I didn't even hesitate to return the gesture. There was this electric feeling when our hands met and I realized he was giving me back all the energy they'd taken, and healing my wounds."

I fell silent again, but she didn't prompt me to continue. It had been the most all-encompassing feeling as his energy flowed through my body. Not invasive or forceful. It was one person genuinely concerned for the well-being of another, and doing everything in their power to help.

"There was commotion behind me, and I realized that everyone that had been drained of their life energy was returning to normal. Kronos, even though he hadn't introduced himself yet at that point, knew I would be too distracted until I was sure they'd be alright, so he released my hand and nodded. Told me he would find me again soon. That we had things he'd like to discuss."

Gooseflesh rose on Meg's arms and she shivered. I lowered my head and she turned hers upward just in time to meet me for a kiss. That was the first time I'd met a Titan, and now, thousands of years in the making, the journey that had started that day was at its final resolution. And the Fates had seen fit to bless us with this incredible mate in the process. I pulled away and she groaned, following for another kiss, which I gladly gave.

I would have liked to have given her more, but I was still healing. It probably wouldn't hurt, but I wouldn't be able to give it my best effort, which was worse in my eyes. When we finally broke apart, breathless, she asked, "Did everyone in your outfit make it?"

I shook my head. "No. Some of them were already dead, there would be no saving them. But most were fine. Eventually. A lot of them had difficulty dealing with what happened and left the company anyway. The likelihood of that happening again may have been slim, but it was a lot for anyone to comprehend. That whole town eventually dispersed, falling to ruins. They called it a cursed place."

"We were marching through Etruria, on the way to quash a small uprising with some newly acquired territory. The local merchants were angry at the tithes, nothing new. But it turned into an ambush. They'd lured us there and meanwhile had troops from an enemy state waiting for us. It was dirty and underhanded, and they got their victory. I was alone again, wandering again. The few others that had managed to escape disappeared into the wilderness. I never saw them again.

"As I was walking through a sparse desert region, I think I'd made it to Carthage at that point, there had been no sign of a settlement for days. I'd only found one well that was almost completely dried up. There had been a village around it, but it had long ago packed up and moved on. I'd had no food for days and I was hopelessly lost."

"That's when he found you," she said.

"Yes. Kronos appeared, not in his full manifestation, but he was still a sight to behold. He brought Rhea and Pallas with him. They transported me to a grand place in a green countryside and sat down with me at the same table, making sure I had my fill of food and drink. That's where I met Gareth, Remi and Hadi for the first time."

"Where they making you an offer? Why would they bring you there?"

"They began to outline their ideas, creating a small band of elite Strangers that embodied certain qualities they admired. Strength, honesty, valor, loyalty. We would be their emissaries on the ground, go where they could not. Talk to people who would otherwise be too afraid to speak to them in a candid manner. They aspired to get mortals and Strangers alike on the same page, united against the Ætherim that were posing an increasing threat. The power had gone to the gods' heads. They were falling into the same traps that their ancestors had, and the Titans knew that if it took another turn in that direction, the world wouldn't survive a second time. Prometheus had become rather fond of the people populating this planet. When the gods captured him and turned him against us, the Titans knew they had no choice but to act or risk losing everything."

"How could you possibly make that kind of decision?" Meg asked, staring out over the water. She was shaking her head, puzzling out the circumstances. "If I'd been offered the task of helping them, I don't think any part of me would've wanted to join them."

"I know it's hard for you to believe, but when you meet them yourself someday, you'll understand. They have a way of instilling you with such confidence, like you can conquer the world."

She frowned and recoiled, so I elaborated. "Maybe a bad choice of words. They seem nothing but genuine. They can be terrifying, especially if their anger is directed at you. But at no time did I ever expect any of them to be capable of brash, unwarranted violence just for the sake of it.”

“Unlike a certain ancient god that takes everything as a personal affront to his superiority,” she said.

I stifled a yawn, and she caught it. “You need sleep, and I just keep asking questions.”

“Don’t apologize. We’ve got a lot to learn about each other.”

She bowed her head and pulled me up. “Sleep. Then we can travel on and find Gareth in the morning.” She bit her lip. “At least I hope so.”

We moved over to her makeshift bedding, and she curled into me. I waited until she fell asleep, just listening to her even breaths and the soft sighs that would escape now and then. She’d pulled me out of my hell when I was under that curse. There wasn’t a single thing on this earth or any other I wouldn’t do to keep her safe.

Meg looked so delicate in my arms, her hand tucked under her chin. A fierce warrior spirit in the body of a porcelain doll. I still had trouble wrapping my head around it. The Fates had a funny way of disguising great power in unassuming vessels. And I couldn’t wait to see just what they had in store for us all.

I woke to find Meg up and moving about the ship, stretching her body in ways that brought out my feral need to claim her. It was a shame that we hadn’t been able to bond. The true-mate connection is just so much deeper, and I hoped I wouldn’t wind up resenting Gareth for having the honor.

“Are you ready?” I asked her.

"Sure am," she said. "The question is, are *you* ready?" A teasing grin lit up her face. "You've clearly already traveled this way in some capacity, but it might be a whole different experience with me."

"I trust you," I said, getting to my feet and working the knots out of my muscles. The rest of my injuries had healed, but I was aware of exactly where they'd been. "What do you need from me?"

A hungry glint flashed through her eyes, but she shook her head. "Maybe later."

"Definitely later," I said, telling my cock to calm down.

"When Gareth and I did this," she frowned. "The bond had—formed differently—but, he essentially just passed his energy into me and bolstered my power so I could move us. The block is probably my mind playing a mean trick, but with you to support me, I think I can get past it."

I rested my hands on her shoulders. "I know you can. But I think I have a suggestion of how we can utilize the bond a different way. Do you remember when I bit you? The sensations that came with it?"

She drew in a ragged breath and I noticed her thighs clench together. I grinned. "Clearly, you do. And if you're indeed being blocked by your own fears, it'll give you a distraction."

Meg nodded and tilted her head to the side. My lips brushed her skin, the pulse jumping in her veins. I breathed in the scent of her and my pupils dilated. She was intoxicating.

"Ready?" I whispered against her throat.

"Yes." Her hands ran through my hair and gripped me tight.

My incisors lengthened, and I ran my tongue over her before sinking my fangs in. Her blood spurted into my mouth, hot and sweet, and she gasped before crying out, shuddering with climax. My arms wrapped tightly around her as her knees shook.

Her power was building around us, and I took another pull of her blood, pouring my own power into her as I did so. A million pinpricks rushed over my skin and the world dissolved into gray.

# CHAPTER SIXTEEN

# Gareth

Approaching Meg in that dream had taken a lot more out of me than I thought it would. Everything in this bloody world was a perpetual shade of gray. A mist hung over everything, making it impossible to see over ten feet in front of your face, even on a good day. I might've seen the sun peeking through once, or at least it was some kind of bright light that broke through the haze, but it didn't last more than a fleeting instant.

The only sound was a constant thrum, like of a thrashing waterfall far away from here. The ground beneath my feet was dead and dry and gave off a constant chill that soaked through your bones. If I stayed still for too long, the mist would gather on me and soak me through.

I had yet to see any sign of other life here. I spent most of my time in wolf form. There was a presence, oppressive and watchful. At night, when the world around me settled into a darker gray, it would feel like I was caught in some kind of display. A small animal in a cage that was constantly being watched by my keeper.

A truly miserable place, and I couldn't even give it a name.

My chest ached at the wound Apollo had dealt me. Now I had two scars, almost in an X-shaped pattern, if not a little lopsided. Twice my death was imminent, and twice I had been saved.

A new ache rose, and I ground my teeth against it. Being away from Meg was torture. I could still feel her emotions coming through the bond. It was a constant feed of anxiety until pain and rejection took its place, then overwhelming fear.

I'd guessed she'd located another member of our Six when her worries eased and tenderness took over. Then excitement and passion, and I grew jealous despite my best efforts not to. I wasn't jealous of him as much as I was going insane being kept away from Meg.

I'd been dozing in an uneasy sleep when the anguish came through. I'd cried out with the extreme force of it, like another arrow had thudded into my chest. She was flailing, grieving, spiraling. I couldn't leave her to suffer that alone.

Since we'd bonded, there had been a power growing in me I couldn't figure out. It was ephemeral, always just out of reach. I was used to my wolf having his own sentience, but this was something else entirely. A living thing without form.

Could I have actually picked up some of her time magick?

Her pain only grew worse, and I became desperate to get to her. The solution appeared almost like that strange entity at the edge of my consciousness tapped me on the shoulder and whispered it in my ear.

I could go to her. Or at least meet her in the middle. When I felt Meg slip into a sense of unease and quiet, I took that for sleep. And I knew it was the chance I needed to reach her.

Seeing her gave me a small sense of peace, and learning it was Andrus that was in danger gave me hope. He had more lives than a cat, and if he was still the same man I knew before, nothing would stop him from getting back to her.

And of all the Desma she could've found, he was probably the best one at dealing with uncertain situations, adapting and rising above challenges. It was hard to get one over on him, even with purposeful deception. The puzzle-solver of the group.

It couldn't have been more than a few hours after that I felt a burst of joy blossom in my chest. Andrus must've made it back.

Now all I had to do was wait.

The surrounding gray was turning its darker shade when my strange new power woke up again, aware. When I gave myself over to its guidance, I could sense a change in the world around me. Just ahead of me I could see in my mind's eye a shimmering pocket of air. This sight was an unfamiliar experience, like an image overlaid on top of my actual vision.

The pocket bulged and warped, and I knew that something was moving through it from a different place and time. I was watching Meg's magick in action.

I'd seen people transport using portals, but this was different. It wasn't just shuttling people from one place to another in the same timeline. My eyes widened as her magick... spoke... to mine, explaining things to me as they happened. What I was witnessing was a new pathway crossing all plains of reality, regardless of time and space. This magick was bending those forces to its will.

*No.* Nothing so forceful as that. The sentient magick bristled at the idea of being *forced* to do anything. It was a partnership. People who tried to force time to do their bidding paid for it dearly.

The bubble in space opened, like a membrane sliding away.

It seemed to fold back and fall around the two people locked in an embrace.

Meg's head was thrown back, ecstasy written all over her face. Andrus was the first to break their contact, removing his teeth from her neck and licking the wound clean. He tenderly stroked her face, still supporting her in his arms. My mate—our mate—gave a final shudder and her eyes fluttered open.

Andrus glanced in my direction briefly, and then did a double take, a wide grin spreading across his face. "It worked."

Meg's head turned, and a strangled cry escaped her throat. She ran toward me and hurled herself into my arms. I whoosh of breath exploded from me as I caught her, crushing her to me.

"You're really here." She spoke against my chest, her hands sliding up my back and clinging to my shoulders. "Are you okay?" Her gaze was piercing, looking for lies.

"I am now," I said, chuckling. I leaned down to kiss her, and it deepened immediately. Meg jumped up, wrapping her legs around me, and my hands automatically slid under her thighs.

I glanced up and saw Andrus watching us, a wicked grin on his face. "As much as I enjoy seeing her happy, we should probably head somewhere that's less... awful."

"He's got a point, love." I rested my forehead against hers and she took some steadying breaths.

"Okay." She unclamped her legs and dropped her feet to the ground. I noticed she was barefoot, but the cold, hard turf didn't seem to bother her.

"It's good to see you again, brother," said Andrus. He stepped forward, and we clasped our hands together before he pulled me in for an embrace. There was a slight tremor in his voice. "I didn't think I'd see you again. Any of you."

"The Fates wouldn't have allowed that to happen," I said, blinking back my own tears. It had been thousands of years since I'd seen any of my brothers I'd fought alongside. I'd been flung back to the Stone Age of Briton and saw it through to the Iron Age. I'd tried to forge new families, a new pack, but nothing ever lasted. Wolves were long-lived, but not immortal. That was a gift given when we bound ourselves to the Titans' service.

I'd never realized how lonely immortality would be until I was separated from my found family. It seemed Andrus had much the same experience.

Meg was giving us some distance and looking around, not seeming surprised at her surroundings.

"Do you know where we are?" I asked.

She nodded. "You were right. We're in-between time."

"In between?" I asked.

"It's less of a place and more of an idea," she said, shrugging apologetically. "I don't really know how to explain it. It's one of those things that just... is." She looked off into the distance like she could see something through the fog. "This is where I'd come to search for you. Before. Not physically." She scrunched her toes in the dead grass and made a face. "Only with astral projection. As I'm sure you've noticed, it's a pretty neutral place. Not much of anything to distract you."

"Neutral." I tilted my head to the side and considered. "That is a word for it, I suppose."

"So what's next?" asked Andrus. "What was your plan before you got separated?"

"We didn't really have one," said Meg.

I nodded. "We've mostly just been trying to stay one step ahead of Belsioch. That dickface"—Meg smiled as I used her term.—"has been thwarting us at every turn."

"Then let's find a place to rest and plan," said Andrus.

"I'm onboard with that," said Meg, taking both of our hands. "Any suggestions for somewhere safe?"

"Somewhere remote seems promising," I said.

Andrus nodded. "How about somewhere cold? It's been ages since I've seen a good snow."

"I thought you hated the cold?" she asked.

"Only if I can't escape it easily," Andrus explained with a shrug.

Meg was thinking it over and I could sense hesitation. "What has you worried?"

She blinked and looked at me, surprised. I smiled. "You can't hide anything from me, remember?"

Meg shot a glance at Andrus, who forced a smile. She nodded. "I'm second guessing if I can actually get us there. Jumping through time with passengers back to back might be a recipe for trouble."

"You've got both of us to fuel you. You two have bonded, right?"

The two of them shared another strained smile and Andrus spoke. "Yes, but it didn't go exactly as we'd hoped."

I raised my eyebrows. "What do you mean?"

"We didn't bond. Something happened, but it wasn't anything like you and I experienced," said Meg. "I don't know why."

"It might've only been possible with one of us. So you might be it," Andrus said to me, a tight smile on his face.

I frowned. "That seems odd. Maybe we've missed something."

The sadness she was feeling came loud and clear through the bond. If there really wouldn't be any bonding between her and the others, that would be a tragedy. For them not to get to experience what I have with her... that would be tantamount to cruel, not to mention it might foster resentment between me and my brothers. Meg changed the subject.

"I've got the perfect place."

"Where?" I asked.

She smiled. "You'll see." The smile faltered. "Hopefully."

I took her hand and Andrus did the same. "You can do this, Meg." I pumped energy through our bond and she took a deep breath, closing her eyes before she opened them again and locked the violet irises on me. Andrus lifted her hand to his lips and kissed the back of it before running his tongue over her wrist. His fangs extended and I could hear the rasping sound they made as he skimmed them across her flesh. She shivered and my hunger for her flared brightly. Between my rising lust and Andrus's impending bite, I'm not sure how she concentrated at all. I could smell her arousal, which only redoubled my need to take her again.

She nodded, her breath shaking. "Okay. Here goes nothing."

Time wrapped around us, but it felt subtly different from the other instances. It's almost like I could hear a whisper in it as it called to me, welcoming me to the secrets that were only for a few to know.

The world shifted and fell away, and when it next came into focus, we were standing in the middle of a lush green field, boggy ground beneath our feet, piles of melting snow littered across the ground and glittering in the sun.

# Chapter Seventeen

## Meg

Andrus shielded his eyes against the sun immediately, and a small hiss escaped his lips as he pulled away from my wrist. I gasped. "Shit, I'm sorry. I thought—"

He and Gareth were both laughing as I swatted Andrus's arm. "Jerk, don't scare me like that!"

"I couldn't help myself," he said, still laughing. He caught me staring at him, entranced by his laugh, and stopped. "What is it?"

I shook my head, trying not to act like a love-sick puppy. I was standing here with two men, both wonderful, honorable and, quite frankly, handsome as all get-out, and it made me giddy every time either of them looked at me. Part of me still struggled with thinking this was all too good to be true, but time and time again, they'd proven themselves to be genuine. And when I compared how I felt with them to how I felt with Bel, it was a world of difference.

I was at ease with them, in heart and soul. I couldn't imagine either of them raising a hand to me. Bel had his rages before he showed me his true colors, and I always felt a hint of fear that one day he'd turn that anger on me. My gut would always tell me that something wasn't quite right between us.

But there was nothing even remotely like that here.

"Nothing," I said. I threw caution to the winds. "I find myself falling very hard for both of you and I can't quite believe my good luck."

"Believe it. We're yours, for better or worse," said Gareth.

"I'm clearly the 'better' and he's the 'worse,'" Andrus said, laughing.

Gareth huffed and shook his head. Already, I could see the evidence of their closeness. They'd been apart for years, but just like if they'd been biological brothers, they fell back into that slightly contentious relationship where their sole purpose in life seemed to be annoying the other.

"Are we in Norway?" Andrus asked, looking around. "It's more beautiful than I remember."

"Yes."

"Should I be on the lookout for Vikings?" asked Gareth, only somewhat kidding.

"No," I said. "This is way after their golden age, probably closer to my present time than either of you have ever been. 1800s."

Andrus whistled. "I thought there'd be nothing left of the world anymore by then. Kronos himself wasn't sure."

"And the earth is still spinning in the 21$^{st}$ century," I said sardonically. Something about that whole deal still didn't sit right with me. "I'm not entirely sure he was telling you the truth with that one."

Both of them looked at me with wary eyes.

"How so?" asked Gareth.

"Time isn't linear. It's all happening, all at once. We're the ones that put a chronology to it because it helps us makes sense of it, but past, present and future are just labels. He could've looked ahead to the future just as easily as the past. I think there's another reason he didn't want to send any of you forward, but I have no clue what that would be."

Andrus didn't quite look convinced, but Gareth hesitated and his brow furrowed. My eyes widened. "You feel it, don't you? The presence of Time?"

"Is that what it is, then?" He nodded. "I thought it might be, but I wasn't sure. I kept feeling this presence that I couldn't identify. It feels like it's alive."

Excitement overtook me and I bounded over to him, jumping into his arms. He caught me, shocked at my reaction. I kissed him and laughed like a maniac.

"What did I miss?" Andrus asked.

"I'm just excited! I've never had anyone who could understand what I was describing when I talked about Time. The actual sentient being, not the concept. People always thought I was nuts, so I started to think that maybe I was and put the idea out of mind."

I hopped back to the ground and clasped my hands together, overjoyed for the first time in what felt like forever. "What else is going to develop from our bond, I wonder?"

A deep affection came through that very bond, but it was tinted with worry. Gareth was looking at Andrus, who was doing his best to hide his disappointment and failing.

"Andrus, I—"

He shook his head. "It's okay. Maybe there's still a chance for it." He gazed out to the copse of trees where steam was rising beyond. "Is that where we're going?"

"Yes," I said, trying to switch gears. "I came here once a while ago, searching for a link. I remembered this cozy cabin near a hot spring. It should be empty. The ice road that leads here should be too soft to travel on but still solid enough that boats can't pass yet. We'll have it all to ourselves. We can rest and plan."

"That sounds wonderful," said Andrus. He walked toward the cabin, and Gareth and I followed. I couldn't stand to see Andrus hurt like this. There *had* to be something we were missing. Why would the Fates only allow me to true-mate bond with *one* of my mates? We were a team. That little caveat would do nothing but sew discord and drive a wedge between Gareth and I and the others.

Gareth wrapped his arm around my shoulders and kissed the top of my head. "He'll be alright. We'll figure it out."

We breached the tree line and stepped out into a small clearing. Last time I'd been here, I'd had to run from a group of acolytes protecting the item I was after. They'd dealt me a pretty nasty injury, and I'd needed to take the time to heal before I tried again.

Now it was under much better circumstances I found myself in the peaceful spot, secluded from the outside world and surrounded only by the bird calls and the croaking frogs getting an early start on spring.

"Give us a minute to check the house for trouble," said Gareth, squeezing my waist.

He joined Andrus and explained what he wanted to do, and they set off for a security check.

I could feel Gareth's warring emotions. He wanted to reassure Andrus but wasn't sure if there would be any truth to his words. Nor did he want to seem like he was rubbing in the fact that he would be the bonded mate and Andrus and the others would have to deal with always being just a bit separate.

Maybe it was another block that I was imposing on myself. Gareth had been lost, and I'd been blaming myself for that and a whole litany of other things. Maybe I'd hadn't allowed the bonding to happen because I couldn't accept a happy moment at such a tumultuous time.

The two of them moved toward the cabin and circled around it in opposite directions. They both disappeared inside and reappeared shortly after. Then they checked a little way out for any signs of danger before making their way back to me.

"It's safe. Why don't you go settle in. We're going to check farther out, plan for any escape routes if we need them."

"Of course." I grabbed their hands, and we walked toward the cabin before I released them with a firm grip of reassurance.

They both looked at me and smiled and Gareth nodded before they set off on a stroll to talk and catch up on the last couple thousand years.

I watched them go, wondering how you go about reconnecting with someone after so long. They'd still be swapping stories decades from now. And once the others joined us...

My heart flipped and my stomach fluttered as I thought about spending long nights with these men, talking about everything from our various worlds of experience as we got to know each other. All of us settled into a cozy room and sharing stories. After this mission was done, of course.

The cabin was furnished exactly the same as it had been, although I noticed that the windows I'd broken had been replaced with thicker glass panels. And the settee I'd bled all over was nowhere to be seen, a nice-looking couch in its spot.

The room had a small sitting area with a wood-burning stove, small pieces of furniture, a couple of tables and oil lamps. A food prep area had been added to the side of the cabin, like a little outdoor kitchen. I'd have to check on the food stores to see if we'd have anything to eat during our stay. I'm sure Gareth wouldn't mind hunting.

I smiled. We could go together, and he could teach my wolf how to track. But I quickly pushed that idea aside, again thinking of Andrus. We'd need to solve that issue one way or the other. By the time we left here, we'd either all be bound, or we'd have worked through a solution for dealing with the emotional fallout if it wasn't possible.

There was no way I was letting my new family start its journey together with a festering sore in the middle of it. It wouldn't be fair to any of us.

And after the number that Bel did on me mentally, I wanted to be open and honest about everything, even if the conversations were painful.

A quick check of the outdoor kitchen found stores of dried meat and some grain in a sealed barrel that still smelled fine. A little taste proved no mold, and I couldn't imagine them leaving this behind if they would risk it going bad.

It would have to be flatbread, but at least we could have something besides jerky. Although Gareth would be used to it.

On a hunch, I dug around in the dirt nearby and found some more stores of food that had been buried to preserve them over the winter. A hunk of butter and some apples survived their time in the frozen ground, sealed and packed against the elements. I even found a hard cheese that had a very strong flavor I wasn't sure I liked, but it was an option.

By the time Gareth and Andrus returned, I'd put together quite a nice lunch, complete with warm, spongy flatbread that I'd baked on top of the wood-burning stove before slathering it with some of the butter and topping it with fresh herbs that I'd found peeking up on the side of the house.

"You did all this?" asked Andrus, wide-eyed, leaning in and giving me a kiss.

"We haven't even been gone that long," said Gareth, doing the same.

I shrugged, inviting them to sit. "The only thing that took effort was the bread. Otherwise, I just need to cut things up."

The mood was lightened considerably. I'm not sure what their conversation had been about, but they were both much more at ease. And we fell into a companionable chat that alternated with peaceful silence as we ate.

"Do you want to explore the hot springs when we're done with our lunch?" I asked. I tried to keep my tone nonchalant, but they knew my true intentions.

Both of the men perked up, Gareth with his—no pun intended—wolfish grin, and Andrus with the look that had made me nervous the first time I'd seen it, but now it elicited a fire within me that roared into an inferno at the first glance. While his face remained impassive, his eyes sparkled and took on that mischievous glint that promised wonderful things.

The rest of our meal was rushed, and then we headed down to the springs. Halfway there, Andrus scooped me up in his arms and tossed me over his shoulder with a chuckle. "I've got longer legs, we'll get there faster."

Steam was rolling off the thermal spring, a nice sized pool that would come up to my shoulders if I was standing in the deepest part. The water was hazy with the mineral deposits, but it didn't smell like minerals. Instead, it reminded me of the petrichor after a rain.

Andrus set me down, and we immediately stripped. I avoided reaching hands and waded into the spring, eager to soak. The two men followed, and I headed for the small scooped out section where the earth was packed down and lined with smooth rocks to make a natural lounger.

The rocks were a little warmer than the surrounding water. The source of the thermal water must be around here. I settled into the seat and Andrus and Gareth sat on either side, their comforting presence surrounding me with quiet ease.

As the sun moved on toward the horizon, I'd made myself comfortable leaning back against Andrus while Gareth absent-mindedly rubbed my feet and calves.

"It's so peaceful here," I murmured.

Andrus's hand was moving in slow strokes across my abdomen. I caught Gareth's eye and hunger flashed between us. I took Andrus's hand and moved it lower until his fingers grazed the apex of my thighs. He hummed and dipped his head to kiss my neck as his fingers slid between my folds, delving into my opening. His thumb worked my clit while his fingers stayed still and I wiggled my hips, clenching my thighs around his hand while my interior muscles tried to pull him in.

"All in good time," he purred against my neck, thumb pressing harder and circling. A thrill of pleasure sang through me, and I bit back a moan.

"No, love. We want to hear you," said Gareth. His voice was strained and I could feel how difficult it was for him to wait.

The sharp points of Andrus's teeth slid against my pulse while he simultaneously massaged my inner walls, adding a third finger while his thumb continued in slow circles. I gasped.

"More," I whispered. "Please."

"Should we give her more?" Andrus asked Gareth, a teasing tone in his voice.

"Aye, we should."

Andrus removed his fingers and passed me over to Gareth. I straddled him on my knees and wrapped my arms around his neck, kissing him deeply. I heard the splash of water and Andrus's hands wrapped around my hips, pulling me up into an all-fours position. Gareth slid down so he could continue kissing me without me having to strain my neck, but I broke away with a surprised cry when Andrus licked up my pussy before his tongue plunged inside me.

Gareth's eyes were ablaze as he looked at me. "Take your pleasure, love," he said with a devilish grin.

Andrus continued to eat me out while Gareth's hands moved to my breasts. He teased my nipples into stiff peaks with his palms and rolled them between his fingertips. I dropped my head and moaned as the first wave of orgasm built within me.

When Andrus whirled his fingers around my nub and pushed his tongue deeper still, I blasted apart, Gareth capturing my scream with a kiss. His tongue tangled with mine as Andrus sat up and I reached back, stroking his face. His lips returned to my neck and his hands roved up my body, palming my breasts.

Gareth sat up and grasped my hips, his fully erect rod brushing against my thigh. The need to feel him inside me took over, and I moved forward, Andrus still wrapped around me, and lined up over Gareth. I sank slowly down onto his cock, grinding against him when I reached the base before picking myself back up and repeating the process.

I felt fingers probe my back entrance and Andrus breathed against my ear, "Would you like one more?"

"Yes," I groaned, throwing my head back with a sigh as Gareth thrust his hips upward.

Andrus pushed a finger past my tight ring and I jerked against Gareth, leaning forward and grinding down hard. A growl rumbled up from his chest.

Andrus's finger slowly stretched me before he added another. I adjusted my angle and eased myself back and forth to acclimate to the sensation. The act wasn't entirely unknown to me, but it had been awhile.

"Ready?" Andrus asked, his other hand trailing light fingers across my neck.

I nodded, unable to focus on forming words, the rising passion already making my head fuzzy. I was riding Gareth at a slow pace and he picked me up, still impaling me on his shaft, to bring us into a kneeling position. Andrus's chest slid against my back as Gareth leaned me forward.

The tip of Andrus's cock pierced my back entrance and I gasped, leaning my head against his shoulder. Gareth's cock was throbbing, eager to move as his hands roamed. His fingers teased my clit as Andrus pushed deeper, the burn of being stretched transitioning into a consuming heat and I pushed back against him, crying out from the overwhelming sensation as both men filled me.

My sudden movement elicited a sharp moan of surprise from Andrus, and he chuckled as he sank the last inch into me. Both of them gave me a moment to adjust, and I reached up, threading my hands through Andrus's hair and lowering his head to my neck. His teeth grazed my throat. A surge of need ran from the tips of my toes to the crown of my head.

"Meg," Gareth said in a hoarse whisper. My eyes snapped to him and he lifted a hand to my face. "It's happening."

I glanced at my reflection in the water, exactly how I had when Gareth and I had first bonded. My eyes were swirling with color. I was bonding with Andrus.

# CHAPTER EIGHTEEN

# Andrus

Meg tilted her head back to look at me and I saw the rainbow of colors flashing across her irises. She drew me to her in a kiss and when we broke away, she smiled. "It's working."

I looked from her to Gareth, and a silent signal passed between us to move. I pulled out and thrust back into Meg's tightest entrance as Gareth did the opposite. We found a rhythm with Meg adjusting her hips ever so slightly to best accommodate whichever of us was sliding in.

Her eyes closed, hiding the beautiful magick happening within them as she gave herself over to us completely, her moans and gasps spurring us on until our pace had all of us breathless.

I could feel the magick of the bond twisting around us, and my heart leaped. As much as I'd tried to tell myself I would have been able to cope without being truly bound to our mate, now that the bond was taking hold, I found I was overwhelmed with joy and relief.

Meg's body was winding tight and when she came with a cry, her whole body pulsed around us, her walls constricting tightly. She writhed and brought both of us over the edge with her almost simultaneously. Gareth and I stilled as we filled her. I wrapped my arms around her as she crashed back against me.

Gareth eased out of her, and I did the same. He moved a little way away and watched with bright eyes as Meg looked at me expectantly. I was still hard and as Meg lounged back against the side of the pool, I quickly cleaned myself off and approached her.

The magick was stronger now as I closed the distance, our lips meeting with quiet ferocity as my soul reached out to hers and cried out in triumph as it answered. A kiss that contained all the hope and passion that made life worth living. A life I wouldn't have to live alone and lost anymore. My mate had found me and rescued me from the darkness, and I'd travel all seven realms of the underworld with her at my side.

In that moment, I felt indestructible.

Meg turned and settled a knee on the edge of the pool, and I didn't hesitate, lining up and grasping her hips. She cried out as I plunged into her and thrust. The magick snapped and crackled around us and she bucked back against me, bringing us together with increasing force.

Suddenly I could feel everything in double, the pleasure raging through Meg, along with my own. I gasped at the power of it. We were both inching closer to climax, and I jerked her hips back to change my angle. She bowed her head and her fingers clutched at the grass, her lips parted in a sigh as my hips crashed into her.

I needed to see her face when we came together, when this bond became permanent. I pulled out and flipped her around, lifting her onto the edge of the pool. Her legs wrapped around me as I pushed back inside, resuming my pace. She bared her throat, and I noticed for the first time the marks of Gareth's teeth in the crook of her shoulder.

I was sorely tempted to sink my fangs into her neck as the muscles in her pussy began to flutter, gripping my cock tighter. But I needed to see her.

I lifted her arm and ran my lips along her inner elbow, my pace never slowing. Her fingers clawed at my back, breasts bouncing with every thrust. My teeth grazed her wrist, and she lifted her head, her eyes locking on mine. Her cheeks were flushed, her breaths coming in short pants. She moaned and her eyes drifted closed, but my intense gaze brought them back around to me. When our eyes locked, I sank my teeth into her wrist.

The magick crashed over us as the bond solidified. Meg screamed her release, and I slammed home, filling her once more. We both shuddered and gasped, pressed tightly together until the last of the shaking stopped and we caught our breaths.

We shared a tender kiss, for the first time as fully bonded mates, and I could feel her emotions as if they were my own. I cleared the damp hair from her face and placed a kiss on her forehead.

"My savior," I whispered.

Her fingernails scratched at the stubble on my chin. "I'm no savior," she said. "You found your own way back. I just turned the porch light on."

"Porch light?" I asked.

"It's a modern torch for your door," she explained, grinning. Her incisors elongated in a flash, and she yelped as they pierced her lip. She clapped a hand to her mouth and laughed.

I lowered her hand and licked the blood off the already closing wounds as her teeth slid back to normal.

"I look forward to teaching you how to use those," I murmured.

Another sweet kiss and we separated. Only then did Gareth approach. He was still erect as well and Meg reached out so casually, gripping his cock and rubbing her thumb across the tip before stroking him to release. I gasped as he came, able to feel it through the bond we all three now shared.

Things were about to get very interesting indeed.

"Do you know exactly where the others are?" I asked. "Or is it just a vague sense?"

"Unless they've made significant moves, I should know right where to find them," said Meg, her hair still damp from our time in the springs. The sudden urge to run my hands through it again, watch her as she swallowed my cock, blasted through me and her eyes glinted as she felt it. Her hand settled on my thigh and squeezed.

I hadn't let myself believe it had actually worked. But now, as she clearly knew exactly what I was thinking, it seemed to really hit home. I'd bonded with my mate. We'd figured out the solution, even though we hadn't been trying to, and now Meg and Gareth's duet had become our triad.

I could feel Gareth's emotions as well, even though it seemed like they were only echoes passed through Meg. It might be problematic at times, but it would certainly keep us honest with one another.

I realized he was looking at me, clearly expecting an answer. I blinked and looked around at him. "Sorry?"

He smirked but didn't acknowledge the moment I'd been so enraptured by our mate that I'd blocked out everything else.

"I asked what you think the best course of action is?" he repeated. "With us in tow, she should have plenty of power to transport all of us. We jump to the others, snatch them up and get everyone to a safe location. Go from there."

I nodded. "That might be an option. As long as we're moving fast enough that Belsioch doesn't throw anything at us in between."

"And the other options?" Meg asked.

"We go on the offensive. Port to each location with the intention of holding our position and getting Belsioch to be the one scrambling. I think that will put us in a much better position when the final battle comes around."

A knock on the back door made all of us pause and turn.

"Are we expecting someone?" asked Gareth.

Meg shot him a look that plainly said he was being ridiculous. I took a step forward to check the side door when both doors burst open. I leaped back to stand in front of Meg, Gareth right next to me, a barrier against whatever was coming through that door. I heard a *whoosh* and tackled Meg to the floor, a knife sailing over us right where her head would've been.

A single man stood at the side door, his face impassive. A man and a woman stood at the front, wearing the same—uniform?—as the other.

All three of them radiated a deadly, vicious power. There was no doubt what they were here for.

Gareth leaped to attack and, in the blink of an eye, he was down. Rivulets of blood trickled over him. There had been no sound, no movement from the three creatures at the doors, but Gareth was lying motionless on the floor.

I got slowly to my feet and helped Meg up after me, keeping her firmly tucked behind my body. Our newly forged bond pulsed with wariness. Neither of us had any clue what these creatures were. How do you fight something if you have no idea what its weaknesses are?

The three figures still stood in silence, making no move toward us. The waiting was even worse than an attack.

"What do you want?" Meg asked.

The smallest hint of a smile played across all three of their faces in unison. But they remained silent.

A bird trilled in the distance, and in a blink the three of them surrounded us, their power pressed in so close it made me sick to my stomach.

My head pounded and my heartbeat raced. Meg clutched tightly to my hand, staring at Gareth on the floor, looking for any sign of life.

I studied the new arrivals. "We've met before."

Meg inhaled sharply, and I felt her gaze bore into me.

One of the male figures, the taller one, made a slight shift of his shoulders. So that was a yes. "The Hounds."

Our only choice was escape. We couldn't fight these things.

Meg drew on her power and the Hounds snapped their attention to her.

"Where do you think you're going?" asked the woman. "We've only just got here."

She paused and shrugged. "Anywhere but here seems like a good choice."

The woman smiled. "At least you're honest."

I stared at her. "Do I need to ask who sent you?" Instead of feeling fear, the only thing I felt in that moment was pure rage. Belsioch couldn't get us himself, so he sent assassins to do the job for him. I wondered what it had cost him? Beasts like these didn't work for cheap, and they had no allegiances to call on.

Meg's mind was working furiously as she tried to figure a way out.

*...maybe I could try to send them to a shadow realm like I'd done to Gareth? I'm still not sure how I did it, but if I just hit them with my magic and hope for the best...*

I started and had to check myself before I turned my back on the monsters in front of me to stare at my mate.

*Probably not the best choice.*

Was I hearing her thoughts? *Am I hearing your thoughts?*

Meg's mind quieted as she was startled into silence. Her hand gripped me tighter.

*Andrus?* she thought.

*Yes,* I answered.

She didn't waste time embracing the weird, and launched into a full conversation. *They're clearly fast, so maybe if I slow them down?*

*Do you know how to do that?* I asked.

*I'd been able to target my magic to a pinpoint when I was healing Gareth from his arrow wound. Then, I'd been turning time backward. I wonder what would happen if I just slowed time down?*

*Only one way to find out,* I said.

Meg tuned into the signatures of the Hounds and I could feel her home in on the pulsating, oily essence that they shared. I only allowed myself a moment of surprise when I realized they were one entity. If this was going to work, she was going to have to act fast, before their defenses had time to register what she was doing.

*Do what Kronos told you to do. Trust yourself*, I said.

Once she had a good lock on them, she cinched time tightly around them. There was only a millisecond in which their faces began to register that something was wrong. Then their looks of shock seemed frozen in place as their movements slowed. It looked like they were moving under the crushing pressure of the deepest part of the ocean.

We broke past them and rushed to Gareth. Most of the wounds were deep, but none of them had been fatal. He would be fine, he was just unconscious.

Meg drew upon some of my power to ensure that we would have enough to get to our next destination. I took her hand and she gathered Gareth in her arms as she spirited us away...

To land right in the middle of a bustling city street. A horse whinnied and reared as we landed right in front of it, the driver of the cart cursing as he attempted to get it back under control.

Screams erupted from bystanders, and I threw myself over Meg as the horse's hooves came down.

# Coming Soon

The Primordial Embers Series Continues...
Look for a new release EVERY MONTH, six novellas in total!
Look for Book 3 in the series August 28th, 2024

The Death's Left Hand Series:
Death's Left Hand Book 3 – October 8th, 2024
Death's Left Hand Book 4 – November 12th, 2024

Visit gwydionroyce.com or follow @gwydionroyce on insta-
gram and facebook for the latest updates!